'You don't loo
indulge in fand
said.

'Maybe I prefer to indulge in fanciful dreams at night?' he replied.

Spurred on by the urge to match wits with him, she took a sip of her coffee and feigned innocence. 'What you do at night is no concern of mine.'

'Would you like it to be?'

Resisting the urge to grin, she said, 'Depends. I thought I'd worked enough nights lately. There's only so much typing, filing and book-keeping a girl can take.'

'I wasn't talking about work.'

Nicola Marsh says, 'As a girl, I dreamed of being a journalist and travelling the world in search of the next big story. Luckily, I have had the opportunity to travel the world, but my dream to write has never been far from my mind. When I met my own tall, dark and handsome hero, and learned that romance *is* everything it's cracked up to be, I finally took the plunge and put pen to paper.

'I live in the south-eastern suburbs of Melbourne with my husband and baby. When I'm not writing, I work as a physiotherapist for a vocational rehabilitation company, helping people with disabilities return to the workforce. I also love sharing fine food and wine with friends and family, going to the movies and—my favourite—curling up in front of the fire with a good book.'

Recent titles by the same author:

THE WEDDING CONTRACT
THE TYCOON'S DATING DEAL

HIRED BY
MR RIGHT

BY
NICOLA MARSH

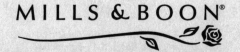

MILLS & BOON®

*First published in Great Britain 2004
Harlequin Mills & Boon Limited,
Eton House, 18-24 Paradise Road, Richmond, Surrey TW9 1SR*

© Nicola Marsh 2004

ISBN 0 263 83855 2

*Set in Times Roman 10½ on 13 pt.
02-1004-36668*

*Printed and bound in Spain
by Litografía Rosés, S.A., Barcelona*

CHAPTER ONE

SAMANTHA PIPER needed this job, more than she'd ever needed anything in her entire twenty-five years. OK, so maybe she'd tampered with the truth, changed her surname and taken a crash course in subservience, but it would be worth the price. In fact, she would have done a lot worse to gain employment as Dylan Harmon's butler.

'So, what do you think?' Sam pirouetted in front of her best friend, Ebony.

'Honestly? I think you're nuts.'

'Why? Doesn't the uniform fit? Does it make my backside look too big?'

Ebony rolled her eyes and snorted. 'Oh yeah, like anything could make you look huge! Puhlease!'

Sam sat down on the part of anatomy in question. 'You're probably right. I am nuts but this is what I want to do. The least you can do is support me.'

Ebony wrapped an arm around her shoulders and squeezed. 'Hey, who's been your biggest fan all these years? And who gave you a crash course in ''bowing and scraping, butler-style''? Not to mention a glowing reference.'

Sam smiled. 'Point taken. Let's just hope that I remember your tips when it comes to the crunch.'

'Oh, when's that? When the dashing Dylan asks you to hold his warmed towel as he steps from a hot shower, water sluicing down his great bod, from his broad shoulders to his—'

'Stop!' Sam clamped a hand over her friend's mouth. 'If I wasn't nervous before, now I'm petrified.'

'Since when has any guy intimidated you? Supergirl Sam, able to leap tall men and their hang-ups in a single bound.'

'If you're referring to my archaic father and his cronies, yeah, I can usually handle them. I hope Dylan Harmon proves to be just as easy.'

Ebony chuckled. 'I'm sure your five hunky brothers would love to hear you describe them as cronies.'

Sam wrinkled her nose. 'To you, they're hunks. To me, they're major pains in the rear end.'

'Whatever.' Ebony glanced at her watch. 'Isn't it time you left? Wouldn't want to miss your flight and be late on your first day.'

Sam noted the time on her bedside clock and grimaced. 'Wish me luck. I'm going to need it.'

Ebony hugged her. 'You'll be fine. Just remember everything I taught you and it'll be a cinch.'

'That's what I'm afraid of.'

Since when had her life been easy? Sam had bucked the system for as long as she could remember, ignoring the old-fashioned views of her parents who were still caught up in the ancient fairy-tale of their royal blood. So she was descended from Russian royalty? Big deal. The more her family treated her like a princess, the more she wanted to rebel. When her five older male siblings joined her parents in reinforcing her 'duties' as the only princess in the family she'd been pushed over the edge. And the result? A three-month contract in Melbourne as Dylan Harmon's butler, as far as she could get from Queensland, family constraints and their expectations.

What better way to shun family ties and prove her independence than accept a position as some rich boy's servant? Not that she'd told them that. Instead, she'd spun them some lame story about meeting a prospective husband through her friend Ebony and they'd bought it. In fact, her parents had practically pushed her out the door when she'd mentioned the possibility of matrimony to such an influential man as Dylan Harmon. After all, what better way to ensure royal heirs than matching their princess daughter with the prince of Australia's landowners?

'Good luck, honey, you'll be fine. And remember, ring me if you need anything.' Ebony blew her a kiss as she walked out the door, leaving Sam alone with her thoughts.

Picking up her bag and scanning the room one last time, Sam hoped to God her best friend was right. Everything would be fine, as long as she kept her mind on the job and Dylan Harmon didn't treat her like the rest of the females in his sphere. She'd had enough of egotistical, overbearing men to last her a lifetime and she had it on good authority that he was one of the best. Defying her brothers was one thing, gaining the upper hand with one of Australia's most eligible bachelors would be another entirely. Not that his good looks would intimidate her. She loved a challenge in any shape or form and handling the likes of Dylan Harmon shouldn't be a problem.

Now all she had to do was believe it.

Dylan Harmon stepped from the shower, wrapped a towel around his waist and reached for a razor. While shaving, he heard the bedroom door slam and assumed it was the new butler his mother had hired. Not that he'd needed one but Liz Harmon seemed hell-bent on making his life easier these days.

'Is that you, Sam? I'll be out in a minute.'

Splashing aftershave on his face, he wondered what sort of man his mother had deemed suitable. Sam Piper must be a jack-of-all-trades, as his mum believed he needed someone to lend him a hand in all facets of the business. If he hadn't been so pig-headed, she'd have hired someone a long time ago. They'd argued about his workload for far too long and he'd finally given in, knowing that his mother's interference sprang from concern rather than any great desire to rule his life.

Strolling into the bedroom, he came face to face with a woman. Not just any woman, but a delicate waif wearing a navy blue uniform with the Harmon coat of arms over her left breast. Once his gaze strayed to her chest he had a tough time wrenching it back, for the evidence of her femininity, combined with the uniform, could only mean one thing.

'Hi. I'm Sam Piper. Pleased to meet you.' The woman held out her hand and he continued to stare, taking in her short blonde curls, wide green eyes and heart-shaped face. He wouldn't call her beautiful but there was something he glimpsed in those eyes, some indefinable quality he recognised as class.

He shook her hand, surprised at the firmness of her grasp. '*You're* the new butler?'

She gave a quaint little bow. 'At your service…sir.'

He noted the cheeky pause, the twinkle in her eye. 'Call me Dylan. Though it won't be for long.'

She straightened her shoulders. 'Why is that?'

'Because you're fired.' He turned away and headed for the wardrobe, wondering what had possessed his mother to pull a stunt like this.

'If you're looking for the charcoal suit, white silk shirt and maroon tie, they're hanging on the back of the door.'

He stopped midstride and turned around, surprised that she seemed unperturbed by his putting an abrupt end to her employment. In fact, she hadn't moved an inch and didn't seem at all concerned, when most women he knew would be cowering in the face of the famous Harmon wrath. 'How did you know?'

She shrugged and he noticed the stubborn set of her shoulders, the clasped hands in front of her body. 'You're a man of habit. You always wear that combination on a Wednesday.'

His eyes narrowed. 'Been studying me, have you?'

'Call it research. All part of the job, sir.'

'Don't call me that!' he snapped. He strode across the room and picked up the clothes, wondering when he'd become so predictable. 'What are you still doing here? Didn't you hear me before?'

'I heard you but I'm not going anywhere.'

He stared at the waif. Rather than being intimidated, as most people were around him, she met his gaze directly, not flinching an inch when he moved towards her. 'Care to repeat that?'

Sam squared her shoulders and silently wished for an extra few inches. It was difficult to look threatening when she had to tilt her head back to stare her new employer in the eye, though it provided her with the perfect excuse to stop ogling his near-naked body. Her gaze had been drawn to his towel too often for her liking and she needed something, anything, to distract her. 'You can't fire me. I've signed a three month contract.'

A dangerous glint shone from his eyes, the colour of molten chocolate, and she mentally chastised herself for comparing them to her favourite food.

'Contracts can be broken.' He took a step closer, making her all too aware of his broad, bare chest merely centimetres from her own.

Resisting the urge to run her hands over his muscular pecs and see if they felt as firm as they looked, she struggled to maintain composure. 'I had an intensive interview. I'm sure your mother can vouch that I possess all the necessary skills for this job.'

His gaze perused her body, leaving her in little doubt as to what skills he thought she possessed. 'So, you think you've got what it takes to be my butler?' He quirked an eyebrow, as if daring her to agree.

Sam bit back a smile. Dealing with Dylan Harmon would be child's play after facing her brothers' inquisitions for the last umpteen years. 'If you're after someone with the right attitude, the right qualifications and a genuine love of the job, then yes, I'm your woman.'

Her breath hitched as he smiled at her and she wondered where the helpless, fluttery feeling deep in her gut had come from. She'd never reacted to any man like this, especially one who obviously turned on the charm when it suited him.

'Okay, Miss Piper. Consider yourself on trial for the next three months.' He tipped up her chin and stared directly into her eyes. 'But if you make one wrong move, you're out.'

Sam battled the urge to shut her eyes and block out the hypnotic intensity of his stare. Instead, she took a steadying breath, wishing her erratic pulse would calm down. As a waft of expensive after-shave hit her she clenched her teeth, wishing her traitorous senses would stop misbehaving. So the guy had a great body, soulful eyes, a killer smile and smelled good enough to eat? She'd dated better and come away unscathed.

Then why the jittery feeling that just wouldn't quit?

'Call me Sam.' She turned away before she did something stupid, like manhandle her boss on the first day.

'Samantha.'

She knew that tone, the one that most males got when they've been beaten and don't want to give in too easily. So he wanted to prove a point by calling her Samantha? No big deal. At least she'd survived his attempted sacking and it had proved to be a lot easier than expected.

'Can I get you anything?' She fiddled with the clothes he'd laid on the bed, hoping he'd send her on an errand that involved being as far away from him and his skimpy towel as possible.

'Actually, yes. Your first job can be to reorganise my underwear drawer. I want it colour coded, neatly arranged and segmented for every day of the week.' His accompanying smirk, casual stance and quirk of an eyebrow left her in little doubt as to the challenge he'd just laid down. He wanted to make her squirm and, strangely enough, the idea of touching his underwear was doing exactly that.

Heat flooded her cheeks, though she bit back a host of retorts that sprang to mind about what he could do with his underwear. 'Fine.'

'Oh, while you're at it, please choose me something to wear today. *Under* my suit, that is.'

Sam risked a glance over her shoulder. She could have sworn he was laughing at her. However, he stood in the middle of the room, hands clasped over the front of his towel, trying his best to look innocent. She almost snorted at the thought.

Sam stalked across the room, opened the top drawer of the dresser and rummaged around. To her surprise, the first undergarment she laid her hands on was a thong. Leopard print, no less!

Stifling a grin, she hooked it with her index finger and held it out to him. 'Perhaps this would be suitable for today?'

His jaw dropped. There was no other way to describe it, for she'd never seen a guy with so much poise look so totally and utterly shocked. 'But that's not mine!' he said, a look of distaste marring his handsome features.

'Oh? It's in your drawer.' The corners of her mouth twitched as she struggled to maintain composure.

'Are you calling me a liar?' He placed his hands on his hips and glowered as the towel around his waist slipped an inch.

The action distracted her and, for one horrifying yet thrilling moment, she thought it might slide down his legs and pool on the floor, along with what was left of his dignity.

Before she could reply, he hitched the towel up, strode across the room and snatched the offending garment out of her hand. 'Give me that! Meg's been up to her tricks again.'

Sam should have known. Meg was probably five-ten, of perfect proportions and had just stepped off the pages of Vogue. 'One of your conquests?' she couldn't resist adding, though what he did in his private life shouldn't concern her in the slightest. Funny though, it did.

'My wayward niece,' he snapped, 'who takes great delight in tormenting me.'

'Way to go, Meg,' she mumbled, thrilled at the thought of any woman getting the better of her suave boss.

'I beg your pardon?'

Resisting the urge to imitate his plummy tone,

Sam schooled her face into what she hoped was a mask of respect. 'Nothing. Should I get started on my first assignment?' She pointedly stared at the thong in his hand.

'Forget it.' He scrunched and flung it across the room, where it landed neatly in the bin. 'As of now, your duties will consist of business affairs only. I'm more than capable of taking care of myself. Consider this room off-limits.'

Fine with her. The less time she spent around the semi-naked tyrant, the better. In fact, everything about the job had worked in her favour to date and she hoped her luck would hold out.

Fixing a placating smile on her face, she nodded. 'Certainly. Where would you like me to start?'

He stared at her for an interminable moment, before turning away and heading to the bathroom. 'Meet me in the study in fifteen minutes. We'll discuss today's agenda then.'

Feeling suitably dismissed, she gave a mock salute behind his back and headed for the door.

'Oh, Samantha. There's one more thing.' His commanding tone halted her and she swivelled to face him. 'Lose the uniform.'

'Now?' The response slipped out before she knew it, typical of the feisty banter she was used to exchanging with her brothers' friends, who were like family. However, Dylan's response was far from familial.

He strolled across the room and leaned a hand on the door, effectively barring her escape. 'Since when did the hired help get so provocative?' His gaze skimmed her face before dropping lower, sending her heart galloping at breakneck speed.

'Since when did the employer think he could ask questions like that?' She stilled as he reached towards her and ran a finger down her cheek, sending her nerve endings haywire in the process.

'Didn't your mother ever teach you not to answer a question with a question?' His finger dropped away as it reached her jaw and, strangely, she missed his brief touch.

'No, but she taught me to stay away from men like you.' She tilted her chin up, determined not to let him see how he affected her.

'Men like me?' He folded his arms, drawing attention to his broad, naked expanse of chest.

Her mouth dried as her gaze strayed to his pecs, noting a light smattering of dark hair that attracted rather than repelled. Swallowing, she looked him in the eyes, hoping her interest didn't show. 'You know. Egotistical, over-confident, world-beaters. Used to getting what they want and letting nothing or nobody stand in their way.'

He smiled, the self-satisfied grin of a cat toying with a mouse. 'Didn't know I was so transparent. Lucky my butler has a degree in psychology as well as servitude. What other talents are you hiding?'

Sam bit back a host of retorts. Thankfully, her mouth and brain had finally decided to work in sync. 'None. Now that we've got you sorted out, perhaps I should make a start on the rest of that servitude stuff and organise breakfast in the study for our meeting?' She had to escape and soon. Having her sexy, bare-chested boss standing too close for comfort was doing strange things to her insides. Not to mention addling her brain.

The warmth drained from his face in an instant and she wondered at the abrupt change. 'Fine. See you there.'

He opened the door and she brushed past him on her way out, wishing he didn't look and smell so darn good. Just her luck that her new boss would be thirty-something and gorgeous rather than ancient and decrepit like most of the rich land-owners in Australia.

'One more thing, Samantha.' His serious tone stopped her.

'Yes?' She turned to see him framed in the door-

way, looking every bit the consummate million-
aire, even without clothes.

'Welcome to the Harmon world.'

Before she could respond he closed the door,
leaving her with a distinct feeling that while he'd
welcomed her to his world, he'd just turned hers
upside down.

Dylan stalked into his mother's sitting room after
a brief knock on the door.

Liz Harmon looked up from the newspaper she
had spread across the table. 'Good morning, darling. Sleep well?'

With a perfunctory nod, he sat opposite her. 'I
met the butler.'

His mother's face lit up. 'Isn't Sam wonderful?
She came highly recommended.'

'From where? Butlers-R-Us?'

'Don't take that tone with me, young man. What
seems to be the problem?'

Dylan fiddled with the knife-edge crease of his
trousers. 'She's totally unsuitable. Too young, too
feisty, too—'

'Beautiful?' Liz interrupted. 'You did notice,
didn't you, or has all work and no play made you
a dull boy?'

A vision of Sam flashed into his mind, those

startling green eyes staring at him as he'd touched her silky-soft cheek. Thankfully, she'd been looking at his face and not lower, where the evidence of how she'd affected him would have been plain to see beneath the cotton towel.

'I noticed,' he said, wondering if it sounded like the understatement of the year. 'Though what her looks have to do with it, I'll never know. It's her qualifications I'm interested in.'

Liz nodded and gave him one of those knowing smiles, the kind she'd been bestowing since he'd eaten his first bug against her instructions and thrown up, at four years of age. 'She came highly recommended. I spoke with Ebony Larkin, her main referee.'

His eyebrows shot up. 'She's worked for the Larkins?'

Liz nodded. 'Trust me, darling. I wouldn't have hired just anybody to be your butler. I know how much you need the help.'

'I'm doing fine on my own, Mum.'

'No, you're not. Between running the business, inspecting the lands around Budgeree and looking after the family, you're worn out.' She paused and he waited for the inevitable reference to his single status. Predictably, his mother didn't disappoint. 'Besides, you never have time for fun any more.

When are you going to meet a nice young woman to make your life complete?'

'My life *is* complete and I like it just the way it is, thanks very much.' He ignored the swift rising bitterness whenever the subject of women entered their conversations. He'd tried the relationship merry-go-round and had hopped off as soon as humanly possible, managing to get his heart trampled in the process. As far as he was concerned, women and serious commitment didn't belong in the same sentence, especially with females who looked good, had the right family credentials yet lied through their expensively-capped teeth to get what they wanted. Which, in his case, happened to be the Harmon name and fortune.

And he'd worked too damn hard to let his family's wealth fall into unscrupulous hands.

'You don't have to prove anything to anyone, Son. You've taken this business to the next level all on your own.'

'But Dad would've wanted more.' Hell, his ambitious father wouldn't have stopped till he owned the whole of Victoria and then some.

'He would've wanted you to be happy, not running yourself into the ground.' She didn't have to add, like he did.

His workaholic father had taken the word 'work'

to new levels, driving himself to skyrocketing profit margins but into an early grave in the process. Dylan still missed him after ten years.

'Besides, don't you think you're taking the role of family protector a tad too seriously? Most of us can take care of ourselves, you know.'

Dylan rolled his eyes. 'Yeah, sure. Then why is Meg running around placing racy underwear in my drawer? And why is Allie traipsing round the world like a lost soul?' He stared at his mother, noting her wrinkle-free skin, the clear eyes, the black hair with barely a grey streak. 'Not to mention *you*.'

The corners of Liz's mouth twitched. 'Your nieces are more than capable of taking care of themselves. Besides, what have I done?'

He tried a frown and failed. 'You're trying to matchmake yet again. And I'm not interested.'

His mother smirked. 'I'm not trying anything. If you've got romantic thoughts where the new butler is concerned, that's not my doing.'

'The *butler*?' Sam Piper and him, romantically linked? Not a hope in hell. He shook his head, trying to ignore her alluring image again. 'No, Mum, I was talking about Monique and that dinner party you've organised. Didn't you think I'd see through the ruse?'

This time Liz laughed outright. 'You're getting paranoid, love. There's no ruse, no hidden agendas. I just thought it was time we got together with our oldest family friends. If you find Monique attractive, that's up to you.'

Funnily enough, the thought of spending a sophisticated evening dining with the exquisite Monique Taylor and her parents didn't hold half the appeal it once had. He'd grown up with the leggy brunette and had dabbled in a kiss or two once they'd reached their late teens, but he'd never been interested in taking it further. Though Monique was beautiful, educated and attuned to his world, there was no spark to light his fire. Not that she hadn't tried, many times.

Dylan relented. 'Okay, it will be nice to catch up with the Taylors but, just to let you know, there won't be any romance between Monique and I, ever. She isn't my type.'

His mother was no slouch when it came to matchmaking her only son and she latched on to his last words in a flash. 'Oh? Then what is your type?'

A petite woman, with short blonde curls, green eyes he could drown in and a cheeky smile that just wouldn't quit. The thought popped unbidden into his mind and, for the umpteenth time in the last half hour, he wondered if he'd lost a grip on reality since he'd laid eyes on his new butler.

He stood quickly and made for the door. 'Bye, Mum. I have a meeting scheduled.'

Liz smiled knowingly. 'Run all you like, Son, but you can't hide from love for ever.'

Dylan refrained from answering. The day he fell in love would be the day he surrendered his sanity and he had no intention of doing that. He had too much to do yet to fulfil his dad's wishes, the one driving force that kept him going these days.

Him, in love? No way.

CHAPTER TWO

SAM paced the study while waiting for Dylan. She couldn't believe the way she'd reacted to him—stupid, stupid, stupid! She'd known what she was letting herself in for when she had applied for this job. After all, she'd heard about Dylan's charms firsthand from Ebony, whose family had known the Harmons for ever. Ebony had extolled high-and-mighty Dylan's virtues for a full hour before Sam had covered her ears and yelled 'la-la-la'. If she'd heard one more word about the rich, handsome, responsible, caring man soon to be her boss, she would've thrown up.

So, she'd steeled herself for the challenge at hand, knowing that Dylan's looks would have little effect if she set her mind to doing a good job to prove a point to her snobby family. She'd focused all her energy on taking a crash course on butler etiquette, Ebony-style. Thankfully, her best friend had come through for her in every way, going as far as giving her a fake reference when Liz Harmon had called after the gruelling interview she'd endured.

Now that she was here at the Harmon mansion in the posh Melbourne suburb of Toorak, she should be ecstatic. If she could last the distance in this job it would prove to her family once and for all that she could eke out an existence for herself, without their prehistoric expectations for her to marry and produce heirs to continue the royal line. Not that her title meant anything here in Australia; in fact, most of her Russian ancestors had reneged on their royal heritage a century ago, but not her family. They were hell-bent on resurrecting the past and restoring glory to the Popov name. Strangely, many historians here were interested in the Popovs too, which was why she'd had the sense to change her surname when applying for this job.

'So much for obeying orders.'

Sam jumped as Dylan's voice interrupted her musings and she whirled to face him. 'I'm here on time, I've kept out of your bedroom and breakfast is waiting.' She gestured to the sideboard. 'What else did you want?'

He strode across the room and helped himself to a piece of toast and a cup of coffee before sitting behind a large mahogany desk. 'I thought I told you to lose that uniform.'

She frowned, as memories of their intense

exchange in his bedroom flooded back. 'I don't think we agreed on that.'

'You're right. We didn't get to finish that conversation, did we?' He stared at her over the rim of his cup and she could have sworn she read desire in his eyes.

Great. Despite her mental pep talk a few minutes earlier she still harboured ridiculous fantasies where her spunky boss was concerned. He could have any woman in the world and she thought *she'd* captured his interest in half an hour? Yeah, right.

'I thought all your staff wore uniforms.' She tried her best to look demure, clasping her hands behind her back. How she'd last more than a week in this subservient act, she'd never know. For some strange reason this man brought out the worst in her. She felt compelled to trade quips with him, to ruffle his oh-so-suave feathers, to get the better of him in any exchange.

He placed his cup on the desk and rested steepled fingers on his chest. 'Not my personal assistant.'

'I'm your butler, not your PA.' Somehow, the title of PA conjured all sorts of vivid images of how personal she could get with the delectable Dylan.

'You've just been promoted. If you're up to it, that is.'

He'd done it again, known exactly how to push her buttons. As if she would ever back down from any challenge he threw at her.

'So you're that impressed with me, huh?'

He shook his head. 'No need to fish for compliments, Samantha. I've read your résumé and I'm intrigued. Why would a woman with a degree in economics want to work as a butler? And, even better, work for a man with a reputation for being a hard taskmaster?'

She squared her shoulders and hoped that the little white lies she had to tell to keep this job wouldn't show on her face. 'I enjoy a challenge. Working for someone with your vast experience in the business world will be a bonus, if and when I decide to enter that field.' She hoped her answer would satisfy his curiosity—when in doubt, flatter.

He quirked an eyebrow. 'You're not some kind of spy, are you?'

Sam sighed. 'Your mother checked out my credentials and I'm sure you've discussed my appointment with her by now. What do you think?'

'I think that if you're half as good as your résumé says you are, you'd be perfect as my PA. So, what do you say?'

Okay, she wasn't completely stupid. Being Dylan's personal assistant would be a heck of a lot more interesting than bowing and scraping to him and a lot less damaging. After all, she had a lot less chance of seeing him almost naked as his PA than as his butler. 'I accept. Thanks for the opportunity.'

He nodded his approval. 'Good. Now that's settled, let's get started. I need to dictate some letters that need to be sent ASAP. While I do that, you can sort through this pile of invoices. In monthly and alphabetical order please, with the most urgent bills to be paid uppermost.'

She took the pile and seated herself opposite him, thankful for the huge desk. No chance of accidental contact across a great divide of mahogany, though there'd been nothing accidental about the way he'd caressed her cheek earlier that morning. Though she tried to concentrate on the task at hand, she couldn't resist sneaking a peek as he spoke into a Dictaphone, his low tones soothing her. He'd dressed in the outfit she'd predicted earlier, though it looked a heck of a lot better on the man than on a hanger.

Visions of their morning interlude drifted into her mind and, before she knew it, she'd mentally undressed him down to the skimpy towel he'd

worn as he'd strolled into his bedroom looking a
million dollars. How she'd managed to maintain
composure, she'd never know. At least those boring drama classes at high school had been good for
something. Old Mrs Lincoln would have been
proud of her You don't affect me one bit performance she'd given Dylan that morning.

At that moment, the man in question hit the
'stop' button and looked up.

'Having trouble keeping up?' He pointedly
stared at the pile of invoices in front of her and
raised an eyebrow.

Fighting a losing battle with a rising heat that
flooded her cheeks, she shook her head. 'Sorry. I
was just thinking.' Lame, even by her standards,
but what could she do when the object of her lust-
ful fantasy was glaring at her with those dark eyes
that screamed, Come and get me?

'About what? Some old boyfriend you've left
behind in Sydney?'

'I'm not from Sydney.' She responded without
thinking and, predictably, he pounced on her answer.

'But I thought you'd been working for the
Larkins?' His stare intensified, leaving her squirm-
ing like a bug under a ten-year-old's magnifying
glass in the sun.

Crossing her fingers behind her back, she hoped her voice remained steady. 'I was, but I'm from Brisbane originally.'

'Ah.' Before she could breathe a sigh of relief, he continued, 'So, what about the boyfriend?'

For a moment, she hoped he was asking out of interest in her as an available woman, before reality set in. The likes of Dylan Harmon would never be interested in the hired help, unless it was for one thing. And she had no intention of making that bed or lying in it.

'You're my boss, not my owner. My private life is none of your business.' She folded her arms in a purely defensive gesture, wishing she could ignore that probing stare. Unfortunately, her action drew his stare downwards before he quickly returned his gaze to her face.

'That's where you're wrong. You'll be spending a lot of time travelling between our outback property and Melbourne, with little time off for socialising. I need to know that you're one hundred per cent committed to this job. Otherwise, I'll find someone else.' He picked up a pen and tapped it against the desk, as though impatiently awaiting her answer.

Though it went against the grain, she had to tell him about her private life—or lack of one. She needed this job and she hadn't come this far to lose it now. 'There's no one special in my life at the moment. You'll have my entire focus for the time I'm employed.'

His face softened at her response. 'Good. I need all your attention…for the tasks at hand.'

His pause, combined with the subtle change in body language as he leaned towards her, sent her imagination spiralling out of control again. She stared at him, caught in the hypnotic intensity of his smouldering eyes, wanting to look away yet powerless to do so. If she didn't know better, she could have sworn that he felt the bizarre attraction she'd conjured up out of thin air too.

'Are you free tonight?'

She blinked and resisted the impulse to nod like a schoolgirl being asked out on her first date. 'That depends on you.'

He smiled, the rare flash of brilliance illuminating his face and sending her heart hammering in her chest. 'Oh, really? How so?'

Ignoring her pounding pulse and wondering how she could control her treacherous reactions to her handsome boss, she said, 'I didn't know the hours I'd be expected to work. Your mother suggested I discuss it with you.'

'So, if I say I need you tonight, you're mine for the evening?'

Oh-oh. She didn't need this sort of encouragement. Her overactive imagination was doing fine on its own, thank you very much, without help from his innuendo.

She cleared her throat. 'As your butler, I would've expected to work evenings. As your PA, I thought most work could be accomplished during the day.'

His smile broadened, if that were possible. 'Not for what I have in mind.'

Thankfully, the intercom buzzed on his desk, saving her from answering. She took a deep breath and wondered if he played word games with all his female staff. Was he actually flirting with her or was her limited experience with men rearing its head?

Dylan hit the speaker button. 'Yes, Mum?'

Liz Harmon's voice filtered through the intercom. 'I was wondering if you could spare Sam for a moment? I need to discuss a few things with her.'

He looked up at his new personal assistant, who had her head bent over the stack of invoices and was sorting them into several neat piles as if her life depended on it. 'Sure, as long as it doesn't take too long. I've upgraded her position from butler to

PA and we have a mountain of work to get through.'

His mother chuckled. 'This, from the man who said he didn't need help?'

He studied the way Sam's hair fell in loose curls around her face, the slight frown that marred her smooth forehead, the flicker of her tongue as it darted out to moisten her top lip. He'd noticed she'd done that earlier, when he'd first strolled out of the bathroom and seen her standing in his bedroom, and several times since; he assumed it was a nervous reaction, though it sure as hell drove him crazy every time she did it. How could such an innocuous movement elicit the wayward thoughts he'd been experiencing about what the gorgeous Sam's tongue could be doing to him?

'Dylan, you still there?'

Wrenching his thoughts out of the gutter, he replied, 'Yes, Mum. I'll send Samantha right up.'

'Thanks. Oh, and by the way, you're welcome.'

He smiled as his mother's chuckles petered out and he disconnected. 'Leave those for now. You can get back to it later.'

Sam looked up and, once again, the luminous green of her eyes hit him like a blow to the solar plexus. It wasn't the colour so much as the clarity that shone like a beacon, beckoning him to chal-

lenge her, taunt her, flirt with her, anything to get
her looking at him with more than a passing interest from an employee for her boss. That was what
had prompted him to offer her the job as his personal assistant—the more time she spent in his
company, the more chance she might look at him
with the spark he'd glimpsed when he'd caressed
her cheek that morning. That one, fleeting flare of
fire in her eyes had aroused him more than any
other woman had in a long, long time.

She stood up and he had a chance to admire the
snug fit of the uniform. He had a real hankering to
see her without it—hell, he wished he could see
her trim body with nothing at all—but, right now,
he'd settle for anything else in her wardrobe. For
some strange reason she had too much poise, too
much class, to be wearing a uniform and he didn't
need any reminder of her status as his employee.
If he had his way she'd be far more than that by
the end of her three month stint; it had been far
too long since he'd had a lover.

'About my working hours?'

He resisted the urge to shake his head; ever since
she'd walked into his life this morning, his mind
had been enveloped in a fog that clouded his every
thought. Even now, he could barely remember

what they'd been discussing before his mother had interrupted.

'We'll discuss it later.' He waved her away, noting the stiffening of her shoulders, the straightening of her spine. Once again, it hit him that she didn't like taking orders and he wondered what on earth had prompted her to take this job. Something about Sam Piper didn't ring true and, lovely as she was, he had every intention of finding out exactly what secrets she hid behind that sexy façade.

'Fine.' She nodded before turning on her heel and walking towards the door, giving him free rein to ogle her slim legs and tantalising butt.

Though she'd said everything was fine, he seriously doubted it. Her rigid posture screamed that it wasn't, not by a long shot. And, if his confused libido were anything to go by, he'd have to agree.

Sam slowly exhaled as she closed the study door. She must be insane to contemplate going through with her plan if she couldn't even last the morning in Dylan's company. Heck, could he see how she practically swooned when he smiled at her? And, as for his asking if she was free tonight, she'd had to restrain herself from leaping over the desk and straight on to his lap!

Men had never affected her this way; she'd always managed to keep her relationships strictly platonic, preferring male friends to the groping Neanderthals that some of her dates had turned into at the slightest encouragement. Even some of the 'pillars of society' that her brothers had set her up with had turned out to be marauding sex maniacs and she'd managed to avoid their embarrassing advances with aplomb. So maybe that made her naïve when it came to men, but did it totally explain her over-the-top reaction to Dylan?

What made him so special that every self-preservation mechanism she'd ever used seemed to malfunction whenever he so much as looked at her? Whatever it was, she needed to get a handle on it quick smart. Heck, that was all she needed, her new boss to think she had some childish crush on him.

Taking a deep breath, she knocked on the door to Liz Harmon's sitting room.

'Come in, Sam.'

Sam opened the door, wondering what the older woman could want. After the initial interview they hadn't crossed paths, though she'd taken an instant liking to the elegant Liz.

'You wanted to see me, Mrs Harmon?'

Liz waved towards a chair. 'Take a seat, child. And please, call me Liz.'

Keeping her surprise from showing, Sam perched on the overstuffed chair and folded her hands in her lap.

Liz reached for a leather-bound book on a nearby table and opened it. 'I know all about you, dear.'

She fixed Sam with a piercing stare, leaving her in little doubt as to what she meant. Sam clenched her hands till the knuckles whitened, trying to buy valuable time to compose an answer that wouldn't incriminate yet sounded honest at the same time.

However, Liz continued before she had the chance to speak. 'There was something about you that looked familiar at the interview, so I followed a hunch. I'm a great fan of history, you know.'

In that instant, any hope Sam harboured that the older lady was just fishing for information vanished. Schooling her features into a polite mask, she said, 'I can explain—'

'Please.' Liz held up her hand. 'Indulge an old lady for a moment.' She flicked a few pages before stopping at what looked like a family tree and tracing a line with her finger. 'You must be Princess Samantha Popov. Am I correct?' She looked up expectantly, not a trace of anger on her face.

Sam didn't know where to look, an embarrassed heat flooding her cheeks. She'd been caught out in her lie and on the first day! She nodded, not quite understanding the excited look on the other woman's face. 'You're right. I'm sorry for lying to you but I really needed this job.' She stood quickly, wishing the Persian rug beneath her feet would disappear and the ground underneath would open up and swallow her. 'I'll pack my things and be out of your way as soon as possible.'

Liz slammed the book shut, sending a cloud of dust into the air. 'Don't be hasty, child. We have so much to talk about.'

Sam shook her head in bewilderment. If Liz had appeared excited a moment ago, she now looked downright ecstatic. 'I don't understand. You want me to stay?'

Liz waved her back to the chair she'd just vacated. 'Of course. I'm sure you had a very good reason for lying to obtain this job and I want to hear it. I also want to hear every last detail of your story, without a single omission.'

'So, I'm not fired?' Sam held her breath, praying for a miracle yet knowing they rarely happened, at least to her.

'Fired? My dear, you've just made my day.'

'How so?'

Liz grinned, the expression on her face rivalling that of a child on Christmas Day. 'If my son thought finding an attractive woman as his butler was a surprise, wait till he finds out I chose him a princess to boot!'

Sam's heart plummeted. If Dylan found out her background she'd be out of the Harmon mansion so fast her head would spin. She needed to stay, at least till the trial three months were up. Anything less and her family wouldn't be convinced she could make it on her own and she'd be back to square one, enduring their rigid conditions and stipulations regarding her life.

Right now, she needed to convince Liz Harmon that keeping her identity a secret was the best thing for all concerned, even if it meant keeping it from her precious son. Taking a steadying breath, she looked up and met the older lady's gaze directly. Seeing the twinkle in her eye, she hoped to God that Liz wanted in on the secret, otherwise she'd be back in Brisbane and pledged to some ancient groom before she could blink.

Tied to some fossil in matrimony because it suited her royal parents and their antiquated ideas? Uh-uh.

Liz leaned forward. 'Start at the beginning, dear. And tell me everything.'

Resisting the urge to grimace, Sam did as she was told.

CHAPTER THREE

SAM hated confusion. She preferred order, precision and being in control. However, as she joined Dylan for a late night supper in his study so they could continue working, she knew that her preferences had flown straight out the window following her meeting with his mother. Rather than berating her for lying and sacking her, as she'd expected, Liz Harmon had almost clapped her hands in glee as Sam regaled her with a truthful account of her life to date. In fact, the older woman had been only too pleased to keep Sam's secret so she could continue in her farcical role as Dylan's PA.

But why? Sam needed to know people's motivations; it was the only way to stay one step ahead. However, she had no intention of giving Liz Harmon the third degree when the woman had done her a huge favour. In fact, for someone who barely knew her, Liz had accepted her version of events with few qualms. In her place, Sam knew she wouldn't have been as trusting.

'Daydreaming again?'

Sam jumped as Dylan strode into the room and wondered if she'd ever get over the fluttery feeling in her gut whenever her boss came within ten feet of her. In over a week, her absurd physical reaction to the man hadn't dimmed one iota. If anything, her responses made her want to do all sorts of wild and wicked things, such as strip off and lay across his desk! Maybe then she'd have some hope of grabbing his attention, for that was all he seemed interested in—the endless stream of paperwork crossing his desk, taking up every minute of his day.

She must have imagined his flirtation and innuendo on her first day, for he'd lived up to his reputation as a cold, calculating business tycoon ever since. In fact, his love for the family business bordered on obsession and she wondered if he ever loosened his tie, took off his shoes and took a stroll barefoot in the lush gardens surrounding the mansion. By the serious look on his face as he glared at her, she doubted it.

'Daydreaming is healthy. You should try it some time.' She noted the tense neck muscles, the lines around his mouth, the smidgen of dark rings under his eyes and hoped that her banter might lighten his mood.

He piled a plate with club sandwiches and

grabbed a caffeine-laden soft drink from the side-board before responding. 'Who says I don't?'

'You don't look like the type to indulge in fan-ciful dreams.' Heck, he couldn't look any more uptight if he tried. He wore a different suit, shirt and tie for every day of the week, each outfit ex-pertly tailored but boringly conservative and she'd yet to see him with a hair out of place. Except that first morning in his bedroom—though she'd man-aged to effectively block out that provocative memory.

He quirked an eyebrow. 'Daydreams are wasted. Maybe I prefer to *indulge in fanciful dreams* at night?'

Sam looked up quickly, wondering if she'd imagined his lowered tone, the slight husky edge. He stared at her, dark eyes unreadable, as he took a casual bite out of a tuna and mayonnaise sand-wich. She swallowed, trying to ignore the sudden wish that she could replace the sandwich as his supper. She wouldn't mind him nibbling on her, not one little bit.

Spurred on by the urge to match wits with him, she took a sip of her coffee and feigned innocence. 'What you do at night is no concern of mine.'

'Would you like it to be?'

Damn, he was good. Just when she thought

she'd got the better of him, he sent her a loaded comeback like that.

Resisting the urge to grin, she said, 'Depends. I thought I'd worked enough nights lately. There's only so much typing, filing and bookkeeping a girl can take.'

'I wasn't talking about work.'

'Oh?' Her heart hammered in her chest as she tried to hide behind her coffee mug. She loved playing games, especially with a man as sharp as Dylan and she wondered how far she could push it, though every ounce of common sense urged her not to match wits with her boss.

'You've been doing a great job, Samantha. I'm pleased with your work and you've hardly had a night off since you started. How would you like a tour of Melbourne by night?' He devoured the last of the sandwiches, concentrating on his plate as if her answer meant nothing to him. However, she noticed he ran a finger around the inside of his tight collar, a gesture she'd noted only when he seemed rattled.

She smiled, her heart threatening to burst out of her chest. 'Sounds great. Know any good tour operators?'

He looked up and fixed her with a piercing stare, the chocolate depths of his eyes drawing her in, deeper than she'd ever been or intended to go. She could drown in those eyes, spend a lifetime floundering in their mysterious warmth.

'Why settle for good when you can have the best?'

'You're that confident, huh?'

'You'll just have to try me and find out.' He smiled, that killer smile she'd rarely glimpsed since the first day, yet her response had intensified tenfold.

She knew accepting his invitation wasn't a good idea. It sounded suspiciously like a date and she had no intention of getting involved with her boss. As if her life wasn't complicated enough. However, she did want to see Melbourne and what better way than a personal tour with a man who set her pulse racing? If the scenery bored her, she could always cast surreptitious glances his way.

'Okay. I'd like that.' Who was she trying to kid? She almost had to sit on her hands to prevent herself from clapping like an excited child.

'Good. I'll make the arrangements and let you know.' He stared at her for a moment and, from the intense look in his eyes, she thought he might say something else. However, he merely cleared his throat and picked up a stack of contracts. 'Let's get back to these. Now, where were we?'

Masking her elation proved difficult, though Sam managed to keep her mind on the job. She had plenty of time to fantasise about her evening out with Dylan once she reached the confines of her bedroom later that night. In the meantime, she'd better continue doing a good job, for she had no intention of letting him renege on his offer. A night out on the town with a gorgeous guy? It had been far too long…

Dylan sighed in resignation as he straightened his tie. Though he'd been looking forward to catching up with the Taylors, the planned dinner had lost some of its appeal when he realised it would keep him away from the office for the evening. He hadn't felt so alive in years, ploughing through reams of work all day and into the nights, relishing the sense of achievement, Sam by his side…

Suddenly, an unwelcome thought insinuated its way into his brain and he wondered if his renewed enthusiasm for the job had anything to do with the actual work or everything to do with his stunning personal assistant. He shook his head, trying to dislodge her image and his disturbing thoughts from his mind. So what if she'd been by his side, working into those long nights? He'd barely had time to notice her, he'd been so hell-bent on putting the finishing touches on a contract to acquire more land in northern Victoria.

Sure. He hadn't registered the slim ankles, the trim waist, the curve of her breasts, the lightly-glossed mouth… He groaned, wrenching his way-ward thoughts away from her glorious pout and what she could do with it—to him. He couldn't believe he'd been so stupid, insisting she ditch the uniform. At least he'd managed to keep his mind somewhat on the job when her lithe body had been encased in boring navy. Now, with the array of suits she wore each day, his imagination had taken flight, wondering what a stray button undone or removing a lacy camisole would reveal. Though she didn't dress provocatively, he wished he'd kept his big mouth shut. And now he'd invited her on a night out—Lord only knew what outfit she'd pro-duce to add to his sleepless nights.

Another strange phenomenon—since Sam had entered his life, his ability to sleep through the loudest thunderstorm had mysteriously vanished. Instead, night after night, her image filled his head in an erotic kaleidoscope, making slumber impos-sible. He hadn't had such vivid dreams since his teenage years and it rattled him. He shouldn't be having *those* thoughts where Sam was concerned. Dammit, she was his employee! And a valuable one at that. He couldn't bear the thought of losing her so early into her contract. He'd just have to keep his thoughts under control.

A loud knock interrupted his musings and for a second he wished it were Sam, back in her role as butler. Thankfully, he'd had the sense to change that little arrangement—the thought of facing her in his bedroom as he had the first day sent his self-control spiralling downhill. He may be strong-willed but he wasn't a saint.

'Come in.'

His mum stuck her head around the door. 'Ready, darling? The Taylors have arrived.'

He nodded and followed her out. 'Remember what I said, Mum. No matchmaking.'

He didn't like his mother's sly grin. 'Wouldn't dream of it, darling.'

Sam towel-dried her hair, donned her oldest jeans and a cutoff top and settled down to watch a movie. Though she'd enjoyed working late with Dylan most evenings, having a night off was a welcome relief. He'd told her he had old family friends coming to dinner and she'd leaped at the chance to spend some quiet time alone. Since his invitation their working relationship had become fraught with a weird kind of tension. She'd caught him staring at her several times, an unfathomable expression in his eyes. If she hadn't known any better she'd almost think he felt the same bizarre attraction she did, though perhaps it was just a figment of her over-stimulated imagination?

That had to be it. Her last date had been ten months ago and had ended like the rest of them, with her fending off groping hands. So Dylan had invited her out? No big deal. He'd made it clear that it was thanks for the work she'd done, not a date. She'd been the foolish one to put that connotation on it.

Wishing she could stop thinking about him, she reached for her bag of supplies. She'd walked to the local shops earlier and stocked up on her favourite 'stay-in' food: chocolate biscuits, dried apricots, cashew nuts and Turkish Delight. Ebony shared her weird taste in snacks and they'd spent many nights curled up on the couch, watching horror movies and scaring themselves silly.

She missed her best friend, their weekly phone chats not the same as sharing every piece of their lives, as they usually did on a daily basis and had since they'd met at boarding school all those years ago. Thank goodness Ebony had moved to Brisbane permanently after school had finished; who else would have kept her sane all these years if she hadn't had a friend to off-load her family dramas to?

When her hand came up empty, Sam searched around the room before realising she must have left the bag of goodies in the kitchen when she'd grabbed a light dinner earlier. Thankful that the Harmons would be busy entertaining their guests and no one would see her outfit, she darted down the hall towards the kitchen. However, as she rounded a corner near the guest bathroom, she almost collided with Cindy Crawford's double.

'Watch where you're going!' the sultry brunette spat out as she smoothed a hand over her shiny, shoulder-length locks.

'Sorry,' Sam murmured, feeling like one of the ugly stepsisters standing next to Cinderella at the ball.

The beauty wrinkled her nose. 'Who are you anyway?'

Resisting the urge to wipe her hand down the front of her jeans before she offered it, she replied, 'Sam Piper. I'm Dylan's personal assistant.'

Predictably, the other woman's eyebrows shot up. '*You're* the PA he's been raving about?'

Pride filled Sam, though it was quickly replaced by some strange emotion she could easily label as jealousy. This supermodel look-alike could only be one of the Taylors, the 'old' family friends Dylan had told her about. Funnily enough, when he'd said old she'd assumed he referred to their ages as well as the length of their acquaintance.

Sam squared her shoulders, though she fell inches short of the towering woman in front of her. 'Yes, I'm very good at what I do.'

'And what's that?' The haughty tone of Cindy's double echoed in the marble hallway.

Sam didn't like being spoken down to, she never had, and she responded in impish fashion. 'I'm there for Dylan in whatever capacity he needs me. After all, that's the service a *personal* assistant should provide, don't you think?'

The woman's beautiful features contorted into ugliness in a second. So Sam's barb had hit home? That meant that the woman had more than a friendly interest in Dylan and, strangely enough, the realisation filled her with dread. There was no way she could compete with this stunner—not that she had any intention of doing so. The sooner she realised that fantasising about her boss was off-limits, the easier this job would become.

'I think your work speaks for itself, Samantha.'

Sam jumped as Dylan's voice rang out. Mortification filled her as she wondered how much of their conversation he'd overheard. Raising her eyes to meet his, she was unprepared for the appreciative glow in his gaze as it skimmed her faded jeans with the tear above one knee to the expanse of skin exposed by her skimpy top.

'Thank you.' She didn't know if her gratitude stemmed from the verbal compliment or the approval in his stare. 'I'll leave you two to get back to dinner.'

'So, you've met Monique?'

Sam shook her head. 'Not officially. We sort of ran into each other.'

'Oh?' Dylan stared at her, intense, probing, and she had the sudden feeling that he could look into her very soul and see her animosity for the other woman just simmering below the surface.

Monique laughed, a fake sound to match the rest of her. 'Yes, it was quite amusing, actually. No harm done, Miss Piper?' As the brunette laid a possessive hand on Dylan's arm, Sam wasn't so sure about the harm bit.

Right now, she had a distinct urge to harm someone and she was looking straight at her. Instead, she schooled her face into a polite mask. 'Nice to meet you. Enjoy your dinner.'

She hurried down the hallway and into the kitchen without a backward glance. If that was the type of woman Dylan wanted, he could have her.

She would ignore his mixed signals, stop reading more into them than was necessary and do what she had come here to do. Losing sight of her goal at this early stage into her employment would be disastrous. She still had a long way to go to prove a point to her family and getting 'ideas' where her spunky boss was concerned would only prove detrimental.

As the memory of his simmering stare returned, she knew that focusing all her attention on her goal and less on Dylan was going to prove a lot harder than she had initially thought.

Sam snuggled deeper into the cushions, ignoring the incessant pounding that threatened to disrupt the delightful dream she'd been having about her two favorite film stars fighting over her. However, the noise intensified and she reluctantly struggled back to consciousness, vowing to watch that DVD again in the hope of rekindling the dream.

Glancing at her watch, she was surprised to see she'd dozed for over an hour and it was well after midnight. Padding across to the door, she opened it, rubbing sleep from her eyes.

'What do you want?' She frowned up at Dylan, knowing she sounded like a recalcitrant child.

She'd never been any good on wakening, whatever time of day or night.

'I needed to see you.'

She stepped away from the door, letting him into the small sitting room. 'Now?'

He picked up the DVD cover from the coffee table and pointed to the picture. 'Yes, unless you were expecting him?'

Her cheeks flooded with heat. 'Don't be ridiculous.'

He laughed, a warm, rich sound that reached out and enveloped her in an intimate cocoon. 'Someone's got a crush.'

'I have not!' She folded her arms and glared at him, wishing he would leave her alone. It was hard enough spending time with him in the study each day; having him in her room, standing there as if he owned the world and knew it, was not conducive to her peace of mind. Maybe she did harbour fantasies about film stars, but they were unattainable—unlike the living, breathing fantasy before her, who she could reach out to and…

'Are you all right?' He closed the distance between them, his signature aftershave washing over her in a sensuous wave.

She inhaled, infusing her senses with the smell, knowing the potent combination of aftershave and pure Dylan couldn't be good for her health yet doing it anyway.

'I'm just tired,' she murmured and turned away, not ready to face his tenderness. She preferred his bossy, tyrannical side to this gentle caring, which could undo all her good intentions in a second.

'I've been working you too hard, haven't I?'

To her amazement, he reached out to her, laid his hands on her upper arms and turned her around to face him.

'N-no,' she managed to stammer out, as her skin burned beneath his touch. Though he hadn't stroked or caressed, the nerve endings in her body had taken on a life of their own beneath his scorching hands and were firing all sorts of mixed messages to her overheated imagination.

'You're telling me the truth?'

Oh, heck. If he only knew. 'I'm fine, Dylan. How did the dinner party go?' She had to move on to safer ground, grasping for any topic that would wrench her mind away from the reaction of her treacherous body to his touch.

He dropped his hands, leaving her hankering for more. Though she knew it wasn't right, she wished he'd slid his hands around her, wrapped her tight and kissed her senseless. 'The usual get-together. Fine food, fine wine, boring small talk.'

Sam tried to keep the bitterness out of her voice as the image of Monique rose before her. 'Really? Seems like you and Monique would have loads to talk about. Sharing childhood anecdotes, making plans for the future…'

He stared at her, the corners of his mouth twitching. 'Are you jealous?'

'Of course not! She just seems to be the perfect woman for you.'

'And how do you know that?' The twitching had broadened to a smirk and she wished her attention wouldn't keep focusing on his lips.

She shrugged. 'Call it intuition.'

He took a step closer, once again invading her personal space and sending her pulse racing. 'Monique is not my type.'

Sam knew he was baiting her. She knew she shouldn't ask the next question. However, with his dark eyes hypnotically boring into hers and his body standing so close she could feel the heat radiating off it, she went ahead and did it anyway.

'What is your type?' she asked, soft and breathy, flicking her tongue out to moisten her top lip.

He didn't answer her question. Instead, his head descended with infinite slowness, his lips brushing hers with skilled patience. She sighed and melded into him, his muscled chest brushing against her breasts, setting her body alight. Resistance was a fleeing thought, quickly discarded, as his mouth closed over hers and he kissed her expertly, leaving her breathless, clinging and yearning for more. He tasted of port, rich and sweet, and she longed to prolong the kiss, the moment, for as long as possible.

For this was no ordinary kiss. Sam knew from the minute his lips touched hers that the fiery reaction of her body, the urge to take this to the next level so quickly, the total loss of self-consciousness, had everything to do with the man giving her the toe-curling kiss of a lifetime. She'd never experienced anything like it before and, damn him, she'd be spoiled for any future experiences.

She pulled away, needing to refocus before she lost complete control and dragged him into the bedroom. Though her sexual experience was extremely limited, Dylan and his earth-shattering kiss had awakened a latent passion she hadn't known existed.

'We shouldn't have done that,' she whispered, reluctant to break the silence that enveloped them.

He stared at her, his passion-hazed gaze doing little to still her hammering heart. 'Probably not.'

He ran a finger down her cheek, feather-light. 'Though at least we've established one thing.'

Her breath hitched as his finger followed a lazy trail along her jaw line before dropping to her collarbone. 'What's that?'

'I know what my type is.'

Sam struggled not to gape as he smiled and walked out the door.

CHAPTER FOUR

DYLAN knew he shouldn't have kissed Sam. Apart from being totally unprofessional, irrational and inexplicable, it made sleep impossible for the next week. Every time he closed his eyes, her provocative image danced before him, faded denim hugging her lean legs and some sort of short top that should be banned barely skimming her flat, tanned midriff. The minute he'd seen her standing next to Monique he'd had a hard time tearing his gaze away from that bared expanse of flesh that just beckoned to be touched.

So what had he done? Made up some lame excuse about needing to see her and barged into her room, manhandling her in the process. Not one of his smarter moves. But then, nothing he'd done since Sam had entered his life made much sense. He'd never needed a personal assistant before, yet she'd insinuated her way into his business, making herself seem indispensable. Hell, he hardly made a move these days without asking her opinion.

Since when did he need anyone's help? He'd run

the family business with little assistance from anybody all these years and done a damn fine job. He
knew his dad would have been proud, though, funnily enough, it didn't ease the burden, the endless
drive of proving that he was the man of the family.
From an early age, his dad had drummed the ideals
of loyalty, responsibility and family obligation into
him and he hadn't forgotten a single lesson. In fact,
he'd spent most of his life living up to his dad's
values and hadn't regretted a single moment.

Until now.

Somehow, Sam's presence in his life had opened
a void he hadn't known existed. Though he
couldn't put his finger on it, she made him feel
ancient, as if he'd lived a lifetime yet had nothing
to show for it. Stupid, considering he owned one
of the largest tracts of land in Australia.

Shaking his head, he shrugged into his jacket
and headed for the door. So much for trying to
ignore her; he'd invited her on a personalised tour
of Melbourne and, though he didn't want to go
through with it, he had no choice. By his own
warped sense of duty, he felt he owed her. And, if
there was one thing his dad had taught him, he
always paid his dues.

*　　*　　*

Sam tried on and discarded several outfits before settling on black evening trousers and a ruby top. She rarely wore skirts on a first date.

First date? Where had that come from?

She wrinkled her nose at her reflection, wishing she hadn't been looking forward to this evening so much. No matter how much she'd tried to convince herself this was just a night out as repayment for her hard work, she couldn't forget Dylan's kiss or the way he'd stared at her every day since. Though she'd tried her utmost to concentrate on her work, whenever she looked up and found him staring at her she lost all train of thought and struggled to give one hundred per cent to her job.

And now, she had to spend a whole evening in his company without the safety net of pen, paper or endless invoices. No hiding behind business questions or typing dictated letters. Instead, she'd be forced to make small talk and, God forbid, face possible interrogation about her personal life. Not to mention the more daunting prospect of facing Dylan at his charming best. If he flashed her that killer smile and stared at her with those chocolate-brown eyes for more than ten seconds, she'd be a goner.

Dashing a slick of gloss across her lips, she hoped she had more willpower than she'd shown that night he'd come to her room. She should have pushed him away and given him a verbal barrage in the process. Instead, she'd submitted to that mind-blowing kiss with all the fierceness of a purring cat. All she'd needed to do was roll over and beg for her tummy to be rubbed, an action she'd been perilously close to doing before she'd pulled away.

As if on cue, a knock sounded at her door. Straightening her shoulders and taking a deep breath, she opened it, doing her utmost to appear nonchalant.

'Hi. Ready to go?'

Ready and raring.

Dylan smiled and, for a horrifying second, she wondered if she'd spoken aloud. However, he continued to stare at her, obviously awaiting her answer.

She nodded, wishing her heart would stop hammering a staccato beat. 'Lead the way.'

'The view's that good, huh?' His grin broadened and she wished she'd had the sense to refuse his invitation.

Fighting a rising blush and losing, she brushed past him and stalked ahead. 'I wouldn't know. Haven't really checked it out.'

His chuckles followed her down the hallway and

out to the car, where she leaned against the door and tried her best to look nonchalant.

'By the way, you look great.' He opened the passenger door for her, a waft of woody aftershave washing over her and sending her already reeling senses spiralling dangerously out of control. 'And, from where I stand, the view is sensational.'

Sam didn't reply, knowing she'd say something incriminating, like, Take me, I'm yours. Instead, she muttered her thanks as he slid into the car and she fished around for a safe topic of conversation.

'So, where are we off to?'

'Dinner at Southbank, a cruise up the Yarra, coffee on the observation deck of the Rialto. And anything else that takes your fancy.'

She risked a quick glance at his face, noting the relaxed lines, the slight smile tugging at the corners of his mouth. She'd never seen him this laid back and it scared her; if she couldn't resist him at his stern, business best, she had no hope with this new, appealing Dylan.

'Let's just take it as it comes, okay?'

'Sounds good to me.'

He drove with the expertise of a man used to handling the large recreational vehicle and she wondered if he was bad at anything. She'd never met a man who exuded such charisma, such confidence, in everything he did. If he ever turned his expertise to seducing her, she'd be a pushover.

He pointed out several landmarks as he drove, saving her from making conversation. Not that she could have strung more than two sensible words together; if she thought working in the confines of a study was hard, being enclosed in a motor vehicle with a man who smelled good enough to eat was doing strange things to her insides.

Unfortunately, once they were settled at an intimate table for two at a plush seafood restaurant, had ordered their meal and had their wine glasses filled, he refocused his attention on her.

'So, tell me the Samantha Piper story.'

Almost choking on her wine, she cleared her throat and made a lightning-fast decision to stick to as much of the truth as possible. 'Not much to tell. I come from a fairly conservative family, with five brothers who are major pains. I've done a degree but I'd prefer to get some hands-on life experience before I pursue a career in the field.'

'Five brothers? Bet your dates got a rough time.'

She rolled her eyes, remembering the painful interrogations, the endless probing for information that the few guys she'd dated had to endure. 'Don't remind me.'

'So how many dates were there?' He pinned her

with a fierce stare, as if trying to drag her darkest and deepest secrets from her.

She shrugged and bit back a grin. 'I lost count after the first fifty.'

'*What?* You can't be serious?'

'Deadly.' She smiled and mentally counted the men she'd had the misfortune to go out with on one hand. None had measured up to the man sitting opposite her and for one brief second she wished they'd met under different circumstances. For there was no way she could let anything develop between them, not when her presence in his life was based on a lie. 'Why are you so interested in my life story anyway?'

'It pays to know who I'm working with.' He avoided her eyes and Sam knew he was hiding something. Someone had burned him before and obviously the memory still lingered, intensifying her guilt at deceiving him tenfold.

'Speaking of work, when do we leave for Budgeree?' She tried to sound casual, thankful to move the topic of conversation on to safer ground.

'In the next few weeks.' He sipped at his wine and leaned back, the earlier tension while he'd been grilling her gone. 'Funny, I didn't pick you to be the outback type. Sure you're ready for the barren plains?'

She bit back a grin. 'There you go again, trying to figure out what "type" I am. So tell me, what is the outback type? Brawny women in flannel checked shirts and jodhpurs, cracking whips and rounding up their men along with the cattle?'

He rolled his eyes. 'Nice stereotype. I just picked you to be a city girl. Something in the way you dress…' He trailed off as his gaze skimmed her top, lingering a second too long on her cleavage, before returning to her face.

Sam tried not to squirm, the intensity of his stare sending her pulse skyrocketing. Thankfully, she was saved from answering by the arrival of their meals and quickly focused her attention on the plate of steaming scallops in front of her. As she speared one of the plump molluscs and bit into its juicy freshness, he notched up the heat by reaching across the table towards her.

'You have some parsley right about there.'

She looked up, trapped like a deer in oncoming headlights as he brushed his thumb across the corner of her mouth and let it stray to her bottom lip. She stilled, resisting the powerful urge to turn towards his hand and nibble on his finger. Lord, if he didn't remove his hand this second, she'd do something they would both regret.

'Thanks,' she mumbled, bowing her head and

wishing for longer hair to shield the dazed expression she knew must be spread across her face.

'No problems.' His voice sounded strangely husky and she wondered if he had any idea of the sort of effect he had on her. She'd never experienced such a profound sense of confusion when it came to a man, the jittery nerves, the racing pulse, the hollow stomach. If she didn't know better, she'd swear these were the symptoms of the fabled 'love' that Ebony was always raving about, the emotion that she'd scoffed at and swore to permanently avoid. Heck, if her best friend could see her now, she'd laugh till her sides hurt.

As she mopped up the last of her garlic sauce with bread, Sam risked a glance at Dylan. Relishing the luxury of studying his impressive profile as he turned to gesture at a waiter, she didn't notice the man walking purposefully towards them. Until it was too late.

'Hey, Princess. Fancy seeing you here.'

Sam's attention snapped back as her heart sank. Quade Miller, her eldest brother Dimitri's best friend, towered over their table with a smug look on his face as he glanced from her to Dylan and back again.

She clenched her hands under the table, wondering how much Dimitri had told Quade about her journey to Melbourne and wishing that he wouldn't call her princess. All her brothers and their moronic friends had called her that for as long as she could remember, delighting in the fact that she hated it.

Pasting a bright smile on her face, she made the necessary introductions. 'Hi, Quade. How are you? By the way, this is Dylan.'

Quade's grin broadened as he shook Dylan's hand. 'Nice to meet you. Heard a lot about you.'

'Oh?' Dylan quirked an eyebrow and gave Quade the same supercilious look she'd seen on his face countless times before, the one reserved for people who displeased him in some way.

'Yeah, Sam keeps her family informed of her goings on.' Quade sent another cheeky grin her way. 'Way to go, Princess. So everything I've heard is true?'

Please don't blow it, she silently wished, knowing that one wrong word from Quade could send her plans straight to hell, with her lying soul along with them.

'Possibly, though you know how that brother of mine loves to gossip.' She deliberately kept her response light, knowing he would report back to Dimitri and her family, who thought she was head over heels in love with Dylan Harmon, her prospective husband, as she had implied to them.

Quade winked and jerked his head in Dylan's direction. 'Well, in this case, I think he's hit the nail on the head. Seems like all the speculation is correct.'

Dylan continued to glare daggers in Quade's direction and Sam knew she had to get rid of the other man fast. So far, so good, but all it would take was one stray word...

'Nice seeing you, Quade. Though, if you don't mind, we'd like to finish our dinner.' She sent a warm smile in Dylan's direction, hoping Quade would get the hint.

Thankfully, he did. 'Sure thing. You have fun.' He nodded at Dylan. 'Nice meeting you, Dylan. I'm sure I'll be seeing more of you in the future.'

Sam swore she heard Dylan mutter, 'Not if I can help it' under his breath as Quade walked away and joined a large party at a table across the room.

'Who was he?'

She noted the tensed jaw muscles, the thinned lips and wondered why Quade had made Dylan so uptight. If anyone should have been uncomfortable, it was she. She'd been so sure Dylan would read something into her rigid posture and stilted answers, yet here he was, looking like an actor who'd forgotten his lines on opening night.

'An old friend.' She sipped her water, suddenly thankful for the opportunity Quade had presented her. Though she'd spoken to her family over the phone and tried to convince them that her continued absence meant she was growing closer to her prospective 'husband', Quade's back-up story that he'd seen her having a cosy dinner with her intended would be just what she needed to keep their prying noses at bay.

'Boyfriend?' Dylan almost spat the word out and she wondered at his sudden turnaround.

'Jealous?' She almost chuckled at the notion, but the strange look that flitted across his face made her wonder.

'Of *him*?' He made it sound as if taking on Quade and winning would be child's play. 'Of course not. Just curious, that's all.'

Eager to put the whole episode behind them and get the evening over and done with as quickly as possible, she said, 'Quade's a friend of my brother. We practically grew up together.'

This time, she definitely saw relief in Dylan's face and wondered at the reason behind it. She'd only been teasing about his possible jealousy. Surely he couldn't care about her? No way. She was the one prone to lively fantasies around her delectable boss and if he showed one inkling of interest in return she'd have a hard time keeping them locked where they belonged—in her fanciful head.

'Let's finish up here and take that cruise.' Thankfully, he seemed just as eager to ditch the subject of Quade and the meal ended peacefully, with mundane small talk scattered between the courses.

However, just as she'd managed to replace the lid on her fantasies surrounding Dylan, he went and did something that pried it open.

He kissed her. Again.

CHAPTER FIVE

DYLAN had known this evening would end in disaster yet he'd gone ahead anyway, consequences be damned. From the minute he'd laid eyes on Sam in her slinky black trousers and shimmering red top his caveman instincts had risen to the fore and all he'd wanted to do was drag her back to his room and make long, slow love to her all night long. Ridiculous, really, as he'd never had that urge with any other woman in his past.

Sure, he'd done the dating rounds, but each and every relationship had soured when the women had revealed their true colours. They'd never been truly interested in him, the major attraction being marrying into the Harmon name and fortune. Since the last disaster over three years ago, he'd sworn to avoid lying women. Perhaps that explained his attraction to Sam?

She was a refreshing change from the contrived, artificial women that usually graced his path, from her tousled blonde curls to her quirky sense of humour. She teased him, reeling him in with a beguiling openness that had him hankering for more.

And what had he done about it?

The one thing that he'd sworn he wouldn't do again. He'd kissed her. Correction, he'd devoured her till they'd both been breathless and in dire danger of being tipped into the icy Yarra River. Rather than berating him, she'd had the audacity to laugh!

'Stop it. It's not funny.' His mouth twitched with the effort of trying not to laugh.

Peals of laughter rang out, drawing curious glances from other couples drifting along the river in nearby gondolas.

'Sam!'

Her chuckles petered out and she stared at him with those wide green eyes that had bewitched him from the first minute he'd seen her.

'That's the first time you've called me that.' She'd sobered up quickly and managed to wriggle away from him, putting as much distance between them as possible, no easy feat in the narrow boat.

'What?'

'Sam. You usually call me "Samantha" in that plummy accent of yours.'

'I don't have a plummy accent.'

'Do so.'

'Do not.'

She smiled, the moonlight glinting off her teeth.

'Who would've thought, the high-and-mighty Dylan Harmon reduced to bickering like a child?'

'Must be your influence.' He poked out his tongue like a ten-year-old trying to prove a point.

Her expression sobered as she stared at his tongue, her intensity reviving memories of the scorching kiss they had just shared moments before.

It had started so innocently, with her excited jiggling rocking the boat and he'd admonished her, reluctantly admitting that he couldn't swim. She'd proceeded to rock the boat even more, till he'd seriously thought they might tip into the river. So he'd done the first thing that entered his mind to stop her; he'd reached for her and held her within his arms. However, he hadn't planned the part where she tilted her head up with that playful smile tugging at the corners of her mouth, merely inches from his own.

He'd lost it then, his lips crushing hers before he'd known what he was doing. Her response, startling in its eagerness, had only served to fire his libido and they'd kissed like two teenagers, barely coming up for air. In fact, he would have taken things further if the violent swaying of the boat hadn't brought him back to the present and he realised their predicament. If common sense wasn't a passion-dampener, maybe a dip in the cold depths of the Yarra would be?

And what had she done? She'd laughed at him, loud, infectious chuckles that just begged him to join in. So much for keeping his distance where his luscious employee was concerned. He'd landed himself smack bang in the middle of a situation he had no idea how to extricate himself from. Thankfully, she seemed to have more common sense than he did at the moment.

'At the risk of rocking the boat, how about that coffee you mentioned earlier?' She smirked and all he could do was stare at the slight dimple that flashed in and out at the corner of her mouth.

He folded his arms, wishing that the simple defensive gesture could hold his wayward emotions at bay. 'Sounds good to me. I think you've done enough boat rocking for one night!'

'Spoilsport,' Sam murmured, watching him as he used the pole to manoeuvre them towards shore. She'd never been on a gondola before, believing that Venice had the monopoly on them. She'd been pleasantly surprised when their cruise on the Yarra entailed a trip in one of the long, narrow boats, until Dylan had sat next to her on the padded seat and she realised exactly how small the boat was. If she'd had a hard time controlling her imagina-

tion at dinner, she had no hope in the confines of
a boat with his muscular body pressed up against
her, radiating enough heat to spontaneously com-
bust her on the spot.

And what had she done? Behaved like a mischievous imp in the hope her antics would distract
from the urge to snuggle into his arms. Instead,
they'd backfired, sending her straight to the place
she'd wanted to avoid. Not that the experience had
been unpleasant—far from it. If she thought their
first kiss had been mind-blowing, this one had been
earth-shattering and more. Boy, did the man know
how to kiss? Dylan managed to ignite sparks that
quickly exploded into fireworks, leaving her dazed
and seeing stars.

She floated through the rest of the evening,
barely noticing the stunning views of Melbourne
from the top of the Rialto building while sipping
a creamy latte. Though she'd done her utmost to
convince herself this wasn't a date, it had been one
of the best evenings she'd spent with a man in a
long time. In fact, on a scale of one to ten, it scored
a twelve.

It wasn't till later, when she'd thanked him for
a 'nice' evening with a polite nod of her head, that
it struck her. Despite their strong working relationship, the main common link they shared, they

hadn't discussed business once tonight and her intentions of maintaining a professional distance from her hunky boss had taken a serious nosedive. And, to make matters worse, she had no idea how to re-establish the boundaries again.

As the sprawling homestead came into view Sam tried not to bounce on the leather seat in excitement.

'Welcome to Budgeree,' Dylan said, audible pride in his voice.

'It's breathtaking.' Understatement of the year, thought Sam. The surrounding landscape had held her enthralled for most of the trip, yet nothing Dylan said could have prepared her for the beauty of his family's property.

As the car swept up the circular drive to the front porch, she admired the wide verandas, French doors and floor to ceiling windows that dominated the huge house. Despite its size, it didn't detract from the beauty of the land beyond, towering eucalypts dotting the landscape between native Australian flora.

'Since when did you get to love the outback so much?' He'd switched off the engine and turned towards her, curiosity evident in his face.

'I've been to my fair share of remote areas in Queensland.'

'I thought you were from Brisbane?'

Guilt flooded her; she hated having to lie, especially to a man like Dylan. 'I've travelled a fair bit.'

He quirked an eyebrow. 'You've done a lot for someone so young. How did you manage to fit it all in?'

Heck, how could she tell him that she'd lived most of her life in Queensland, making regular trips to her family's outback properties whenever she could? She'd woven a tangled web and the closer she got to Dylan the more likely she was to tear down the whole deception.

She shrugged and reached for the door handle, eager to escape the confines of the car and Dylan's probing questions. 'Hey, I'm a woman of many talents. Haven't you worked that out by now?'

His eyes glowed as the sun set, bathing them in a kaleidoscope of fiery colour: burnt orange, deep purple and shocking magenta. 'Oh, I'm well aware of your talents, Samantha.' The burning intensity of his gaze scorched her, eliciting an excited shiver that started at the nape of her neck and travelled all the way to the tips of her toes.

She bolted from the car without saying a word,

wishing she could turn off her traitorous emotions. She read too much into every word he said and it would get her into trouble, big trouble. Thank goodness they'd be chaperoned for the next few days, otherwise there would be no telling what she'd be tempted to do.

'Looks like Ebony's arrived,' she called over her shoulder, looking forward to spending some time with her best friend. Though Dylan had initially been surprised at her friendship with a once-employer, he'd suggested she invite Ebony to stay as a chaperon; his old-fashioned values seemed overly-quaint, though she'd welcomed the opportunity. She'd missed their frank, girlie chats, though she'd have to stay on her toes not to let slip her burgeoning feelings where Dylan was concerned. Ebony was no fool and her best friend was renowned for putting two and two together and coming up with five.

'Great. It's been a couple of years since I've seen her,' he said, carrying their bags to the front door.

Before he could insert his key into the lock, the door flew open and Ebony raced onto the verandah and straight into Dylan's arms. 'Hey, stud. Long time no see.'

Sam struggled not to gape, a war of emotions

tearing through her, ranging from joy at seeing her best friend to stabbing jealousy at seeing Ebony draped over Dylan. And his reaction to her gorgeous friend didn't assuage her concern.

He pulled back a fraction and looked her up and down. 'Wow, look at you, *Bony*. You've filled out and then some.'

Ebony chuckled. 'Not so bony any more, huh?'

'Yeah, you can say that again.' He wolf-whistled as Ebony twirled, revealing long, tanned legs beneath a peasant skirt that screamed designer.

Sam stepped forward, wanting to deflect the attention away from Ebony and hating herself for it. 'Hi there, stranger. How are you?'

Ebony squealed and enveloped her in a bear hug. 'You're looking absolutely fab. Obviously, working for this tyrant can't be all that bad.'

Sam squeezed her back, wondering how the green-eyed monster could have raised its ugly head where her best friend was concerned. Why shouldn't Ebony greet Dylan with such enthusiasm? After all, they'd been family friends for years.

She pulled away and glanced across at the man in question, who looked surprisingly smug. He watched them both with an amused expression on his face, as if the thought of two women discussing him was a new experience, one he found exceedingly pleasant.

'Oh, you'd be surprised, Eb. Working for this guy can be hell at times.'

'Is that right?' Dylan winked at her and she nearly fell over. If she didn't know any better, she'd swear he was flirting with her and in front of Ebony, no less.

'We're going to have a great time,' Ebony said, wrapping her arms around their waists and dragging them towards the front door. 'And not too much work, you two. Time to live a little.'

Sam blushed. Funnily enough, she'd already taken Ebony's advice and look where it had got her. As much as she tried to deny it, she'd fallen for her boss and there wasn't one damn thing she could do about it.

CHAPTER SIX

SAM waited for the knock she knew would come. As if on cue, a loud rapping sounded at the door before it flew open and Ebony barged into her room.

Ebony threw herself face down on Sam's bed and rested her chin in her hands. 'Tell me *everything*. And don't leave out a single detail.'

Sam smiled and wondered how she'd survived the last few weeks without their chats. They'd shared every detail of their lives for as long as she could remember, yet how could she begin to describe the strange feelings her boss aroused within her? She could barely admit to them herself. She shrugged, aiming for nonchalant. 'Not much to tell.'

Ebony threw a pillow at her. 'Don't give me that! You're glowing and it can't be the smoggy Melbourne air that's caused it.'

Sam sat cross-legged on the floor next to the bed and stared up at her best friend. 'What can I say? I love my job.'

'You sure it's just the job you love?' Ebony wiggled her eyebrows suggestively and clutched at her heart.

'What else could it be?' Sam looked away quickly, tracing imaginary circles on the plush carpet.

'Oh-oh,' Ebony groaned. 'It's worse than I first thought. You've fallen for him, haven't you?'

'Don't be silly,' fibbed Sam. 'I'm just enjoying the challenge of working as a PA rather than sitting around and waiting for my crazy parents to marry me off to some decrepit old fool.'

'Speaking of which…' Ebony trailed off and Sam looked up. The expression on her friend's face didn't reassure her; far from it.

'What have they done this time?'

Ebony sighed and rolled her eyes. 'Well, that rat Quade told them you and Dylan are joined at the hip and should be announcing your engagement any day now.'

'So what's wrong with that? That was one of the major reasons I took this job, to get them off my case.'

Ebony held her hand up. 'Not so fast, Cinderella. Your folks are saying that if the announcement doesn't happen ASAP, they're going to ''send Max down to Melbourne to drag you back to Brisbane and up the aisle, no excuses this time'', end of quote.'

'What?' Sam leaped to her feet and started pacing the room. 'They can't seriously believe I'd consider marrying that old fogey? I've already told them how I feel.'

'You know your folks. They won't take no for an answer. They expect you to start acting like a princess, sooner rather than later.'

'How did you hear all this?' Sam stopped stomping around and stared at her friend.

Ebony blushed. 'Peter told me.'

'Don't tell me you still have a thing for my buffoon of a brother?'

Ebony shook her head as the rose colour staining her cheeks deepened. 'No, we're just friends. I happened to run into him at a charity dinner last week, that's all.'

Sam snorted. 'You're taste in men is deteriorating, as much as I'd love to have you as a sis-in-law.'

Ebony unfolded her long legs from the bed and stood. 'Hey, it's not my taste in men we're discussing here, it's yours.' She laid a hand on Sam's shoulder as her voice lowered to a conspiratorial level. 'Is it serious with Dylan?'

Sam paused before answering. If she told her

best friend the truth, would Ebony accidentally let something slip to Dylan? After all, they'd been friends for a long time and Ebony was renowned for her 'slip of the tongue' comments. Sam knew Dylan was probably toying with her—heck, he didn't have a reputation as one of Australia's most eligible bachelors for nothing. So what if he'd kissed her a few times and flirted like a pro? He probably did it every day of the week with the women in his sphere. She'd been the stupid one for reading more into it and she didn't need her best friend reinforcing it.

She swallowed and hoped her voice didn't quaver. 'Dylan's my boss. He's a nice guy and I enjoy working with him.' She hoped her evasive answer would satisfy her curious friend. After all, she hadn't lied—she just hadn't told the whole truth either.

Ebony tut-tutted. 'I know you, Sam. You're hiding something. And I could've sworn you wanted to tear my eyes out earlier when I threw myself at Dylan.' She chuckled. 'Why else do you think I did it? Nothing like testing the water.'

Sam grimaced, remembering her earlier jealousy. She hoped she wasn't that transparent; no wonder Dylan had looked so smug. 'Test all you like, *Bony*.'

Ebony's chuckles grew to raucous laughter. 'You *are* jealous. Though don't worry, I'm not interested in Dylan. I have other fish to fry and they're a whole lot more tastier than him.'

Sam seriously doubted that. She'd never met a man who compared to Dylan Harmon. It wasn't just his charm, his charisma or his looks, not to mention the fact he kissed like a dream. No, he exuded some indefinable quality that attracted her, against her better judgement. Now all she had to do was hide it for the next few months.

'So what are you going to do about your parents?'

Sam wrinkled her nose. 'Don't remind me. As long as they stay in Brisbane and keep that hound Max off my tail, I'm safe.' She paused for a moment, then clicked her fingers as an idea flashed into her head. 'That's where you come in.'

'Huh?'

Sam wrapped an arm around Ebony's shoulder. 'As my best friend, I see it as your duty to look after my interests.'

'What do you think I've been doing? Don't forget who got you this job in the first place.'

Sam nodded. 'I know, but I need your help. If you could feed back some vital info, like how close I am to Dylan, how an announcement isn't far off, how happy I am in Melbourne with him, then wouldn't that assuage their curiosity?'

Ebony's eyes narrowed. 'And how am I supposed to do this?'

Sam delivered her *coup de grâce*. 'Why, through your good *friend* Peter, of course. I'm sure you could arrange another *accidental* meeting.'

Once again, colour suffused her friend's cheeks. 'OK, smarty-pants. Maybe I have got a thing for your brother and our meeting wasn't so coincidental. But lying to him? Doesn't exactly help my cause, does it? What if he finds out? He won't look twice at me.'

'Please, Eb,' Sam cajoled. 'You don't want me married off to an ancient crony like Max and whisked away to Europe, do you?'

'As if that would happen,' Ebony snorted. 'Max is as Australian as you.'

'Who thinks like my father, a refugee of Russia's fifteenth century. So, what do you say? Will you do it?'

A mischievous gleam shone from Ebony's dark eyes. 'OK, I'll do it for you. On one condition.'

Doubt flickered through Sam. She desperately needed Ebony's co-operation if her plan was to succeed but she'd never been any good at paying a price. After all, wasn't that what had dragged her into this mess in the first place? Her parents, thanks to their old-fashioned European values, felt she owed them and her heritage in some way. And, according to them, the only way to do it was to marry a fellow descendent of the Russian aristocracy and produce a dozen royal heirs.

'What's the condition?'

'You put in a good word for me with Peter.'

Sam sighed in relief. Pointing out Ebony's good points to her Neanderthal brother would be a small price to pay for her friend's co-operation. 'Fine. Though personally I think you need your head read.'

'No accounting for taste, is there?'

Sam heard the uncertainty in her friend's voice and remorse flooded her. Who was she to judge where matters of the heart were concerned? Look at the mess she'd made of her own love life.

She hugged Ebony. 'I'm glad you're here, Eb. It'll be great catching up. I've missed you.'

'Ditto.' She squirmed out of Sam's arms. 'Enough of the mushy stuff. I'll leave you to unpack. See you at dinner.'

As Ebony left the room Sam wondered if she'd seriously lost her mind. Here she was, working for a man she grew to like more with each passing day, lying to her family about the true relationship they shared and hoping that the two would never meet. She must be nuts! *Or desperate*, she thought.

All she had to do was last a few more months; then she would tell her parents the truth, that she'd never really been involved with Dylan, that she'd been working for him and had proved that she could earn a living and eke out an existence without the protection of a man. Surely they would have to believe her then?

Turning to her overnight bag, she crossed her fingers behind her back.

Dylan sat on the veranda, enjoying the cool night air. Being at Budgeree never failed to invigorate him, every sound and scent wrapping him in a comforting familiarity. He'd grown up here, sticking close to his dad, learning the ins and outs of the business that his dad had valued more than life itself. Until he'd grown up, or so he'd thought at the time.

After all, what was so grown up about abandoning the family to spread his wings, traipsing around the world in search of the next best thing? Surprisingly, it'd been under his nose all along but he'd failed to recognise it. And his selfishness had killed his dad in the process.

'Feel like some company?'

He looked up at Sam and bit back his first retort of, Not really. Funnily enough, she fitted in around here, a fact that had surprised him. It wasn't her worn jeans, denim shirts or leather boots that gave him that impression; instead, it was just a feeling, an instinct that she genuinely belonged in this isolated countryside.

He gestured towards the rocking chair. 'Have a seat.'

She settled into the chair, the creaking wood reminding him of nights long ago when he used to perch on his mum's lap and she'd tell him wonderful stories about bunyips and wombats, while the night sounds of hooting owls and wheezing possums lulled him to sleep.

'You look like you're doing some serious thinking.'

'Just old memories.' He gazed out at the growing darkness, wishing it didn't feel so damn comfortable to be sitting here with her. He didn't want to feel this way where Sam was concerned. She'd be out of his life sooner rather than later and he'd had enough of losing people who mattered to him.

'Sure I'm not intruding?'

He heard the vulnerability in her voice and wished they had met in another time, another place. He wasn't ready for a relationship right now, no matter how wonderful the woman. Besides, he had enough responsibilities with the family and his dad's legacy and he would never shirk them again. Look what had happened the last time he'd done that.

He smiled. 'No, it's nice to have company out here. Usually I'm on my own.'

'Not that you seem bothered by that. I get the feeling you're a bit of a loner.'

'Psychoanalysing me again, Samantha?'

She chuckled, the light sound eliciting a response that was almost visceral. Who was he kidding? God, he had it bad. Though he'd done his best to keep their relationship strictly platonic since they'd been out here, he couldn't forget the few forbidden kisses they'd shared or the way she'd responded to him. Hell, wasn't that one of the reasons he'd invited Ebony out here, to act as some sort of Edwardian chaperon? Unfortunately, that little plan had backfired, as the wayward Ebony seemed to delight in taunting him and throwing the two of them together as much as possible. Though he'd known Sam had worked for the Larkins, he had had no idea the two girls were such firm friends. One woman ganging up on him at a time was more than enough.

'You're too complicated to figure out. Besides,

why should I bother?' Her smile lit up her eyes. She was one of the few people he knew who smiled like that, with her whole face and not just an upward movement of her lips.

'Aren't you up for the challenge?' A gradual warmth started in the vicinity of his chest and spread outward, making his insides do strange things as he contemplated the ways in which he would seriously like to challenge her. Starting with more eager responses from her luscious lips…

'I thrive on a challenge. Thought you'd have figured that out by now.' She fixed him with an indescribable stare from her cat-like eyes. 'After all, I work for you, don't I?'

He laughed, a genuine deep chuckle that echoed through the ghost gums. It felt good. In fact, it felt downright wonderful and he wondered how long it was since this place had heard any serious laughter. 'Touché, Miss Piper.'

A slight frown marred her perfect features as she looked away. 'Tell me about your life here.'

Surprised at her swift change of subject, he gave her the edited version. 'Budgeree's thousand acres was the first tract of land my dad bought here. Though he expanded the business over the years, this place held a special place in our hearts.' He paused, ignoring the stab of guilt that memories of his father and his love of the land always seemed to ignite within him. 'Still does.'

'Family means a lot to you, doesn't it?'

Her innocuous question unerringly honed in on his emotion whenever he sat in this very place and surveyed the property that would belong to the Harmons for generations to come. 'Family is everything.'

'But don't you ever feel stifled? Or need to run away?' He heard something in her voice that made him look up but when he studied her face the serene expression hadn't altered though she wouldn't meet his eyes.

'Never. Shirking responsibilities is for children. Or cowards.'

Sam's heart sank as Dylan's cold, curt words rang through her head. What would he think of her if he knew the truth, that she was one of those cowards that he'd just mentioned with such antipathy and loathing?

She responded more sharply than intended. 'Not everyone is cut out for shouldering the burdens of their family.'

He pinned her with a stare that took her breath away: intense, probing, willing her to listen. 'I wouldn't consider family expectations a burden. How about you?'

He had her there. She couldn't tell him yet another lie, not when she was living a lie every day. 'Everyone's family is different. Maybe I'm just not ready to shoulder what my family expects me to.'

'Is that why you ran away?'

Ouch! He sure knew how to kick a girl when she was down. She instilled as much calm into her voice as she could muster before answering. 'I applied for a job working as your butler. How could that be classed as running away?'

He shrugged, the simple action drawing her attention to the broad shoulders encased beneath a cable knit and speeding up her pulse in the process. 'Call it a hunch. Even though you said you needed the experience before branching into the business world, I still don't understand why you'd want to work for someone like me in such a role.'

'We're not all meant to be rulers in this world.' She almost spat the words out, wishing she could denounce her heritage as easily. For that was exactly what her family expected her to be, some rich princess to sit upon a pretend throne and order those around her to do her bidding. Hell would freeze over before she succumbed to their wishes.

'Are you judging me for what I have and what I do?' His dark eyes didn't waver as his stare bored into her very soul.

She almost flinched at the icy contempt in his voice. If he only knew that she wasn't referring to the Harmons but her own illustrious Popov family, the masters of expectation.

She stood quickly, suddenly eager to escape before she said something she might regret. 'I'm not judging anybody. Goodnight, Dylan. See you in the morning.'

She walked away without looking back, missing the speculative gleam in Dylan's eyes as he admired her fluid movement.

Sam was hiding something, no doubt about it. She'd just reinforced the feeling he'd had when he'd first employed her and he would now make it his personal business to find out exactly what it was.

CHAPTER SEVEN

SAM knew she shouldn't do it. Every fibre of her being screamed that accompanying Dylan to this business dinner was the wrong thing to do, but what choice did she have when the man she fell for more and more each day had practically begged her?

She thought she'd been clever, pushing him away since they'd returned from Budgeree. However, her little plan had backfired and all she'd succeeded in doing was inflaming Dylan's curiosity further. Though their working relationship continued to flourish, he'd fired several probing questions at her when she'd least expected it, as if trying to discover her deepest secrets.

And now this.

Flying to Sydney with Dylan and attending some big function as his partner was *not* her idea of keeping her distance. Or her cool. She'd barely survived their week at Budgeree together and if Ebony hadn't been there she knew she would have done something stupid. Strangely enough, she'd felt a sense of peace, of belonging, at the isolated homestead that she'd yet to find elsewhere.

Initially, she'd put it down to the rugged beauty of the surroundings and the tranquillity that always seemed to pervade the outback. However, as the week passed in a flurry of business meetings, land surveillance and bookkeeping, she'd realised it was something more. Despite the giant chip of family responsibility that Dylan carried around on his broad shoulders, she'd grown to recognise that he thrived on it and, for a brief, irrational moment, she'd imagined what it would be like to share his dream, his vision, of making the barren tract of land flourish.

'You've been awfully quiet.'

She almost jumped as Dylan turned towards her, wishing the business class seats had more room between them. She'd been all too aware of his proximity since they'd first boarded the flight and even now, as he stared at her with those enigmatic dark eyes, had to resist from leaning into him.

'Just taking some time out. My boss is a slave-driver, you know. I barely have a minute to myself these days.' She rolled her eyes, enjoying the light-hearted expression that crossed his face whenever they exchanged this sort of banter. For a man his age, Dylan Harmon was far too serious. Time for him to lighten up—if that were possible.

'Your boss values your input, that's why he drives you so hard.'

'Is that right?' She smiled, wondering how far she could push him. 'So, is that why you invited me along to this dinner? Because you value my input?'

A flicker of appreciation shot through his eyes as he stared at her lips. 'There are many reasons why I invited you to this dinner.'

Her heart picked up tempo as he continued to stare at her and she wondered what demon drove her to flirt with him. She knew it was dangerous, she knew it was wrong. Yet the gleam of desire in his eyes was all the encouragement she needed. 'Why don't you tell me a few?'

He paused for a moment and she could've sworn that he leaned even closer. 'You're smart, witty and gorgeous, three attributes I value in a dinner companion. How's that for starters?' His warm breath caressed her cheek, sending a scattering of goosebumps across her skin. She was playing with fire and, if she wasn't careful, would get seriously burned.

'Gorgeous, huh?'

'Come on, Samantha. Don't tell me I'm the first

man to ever tell you that.' He took hold of her chin and tilted her face upwards, scrutinizing it with the expertise of an art critic evaluating a priceless piece.

Sam could barely breathe, let alone respond, as his thumb gently brushed her bottom lip.

'You must have men falling at your feet, ready to whisk you up the aisle at a moment's encouragement.'

His words doused her like a bucket of cold water as an image of Max flashed across her mind. Though tall and distinguished for a man of fifty, there was something about the way he stared at her that made her skin crawl. Why would a man that age, who had everything that money could buy, want to get married to a girl he'd watched grow up? Several ideas crossed her mind, none of them pleasant.

She pulled away from Dylan, breaking his tenuous contact. 'I have no intention of traipsing up the aisle with any man.'

He raised an eyebrow at her sharp retort and she quickly softened it before his curiosity prompted him to ask any probing questions. 'I prefer to keep the hordes of men falling at my feet guessing.'

'Oh, really?'

She nodded, wishing he wouldn't stare at her

with those all-seeing, all-knowing eyes. 'Nothing like a bit of mystery to keep a man on his toes.'

'Is that why you won't tell me anything about yourself? Sticking to the old adage of "treat 'em mean, keep 'em keen"?'

'There's not much to tell.' She crossed her fingers, hoping God wouldn't strike her down for telling such a monstrous lie.

He smiled and her heart gave a treacherous lurch. 'You didn't ask if I was keen after the way you've treated me.'

The lurch gave way to pounding as her heart thundered in her chest. 'I treat you as a boss.'

'Yet I'm still keen.' He reached across and squeezed her hand, his touch sending her precarious sense of self-control spiralling downhill fast.

Hoping her voice wouldn't shake, she took a steadying breath before responding. 'I'll be leaving in a few weeks. Do you think it's worth starting something?'

'It's too late.' He interlaced his fingers with hers, drawing her hand to his lips. 'It's already started.'

His kiss burned into the back of her hand, leaving a scorching imprint like a brand. Suddenly, she realised it was true. They *had* started something, yet for the life of her she couldn't figure out what

it was. Mutual attraction, deep friendship or a
whole lot more?

As the plane descended into Sydney, Sam re-
claimed her hand and fervently wished that, whatever she was feeling, it wasn't a 'whole lot more'.
Falling in love with Dylan would be the stupidest
thing she'd done in a long time—apart from running away from her family and agreeing to become
his employee in the first place. But what if it was
too late?

As Dylan slipped into his tux jacket and adjusted
his bow-tie one last time he hoped that this evening
wouldn't be too boring for Sam. He'd attended
countless other dinners like this where rich land-
owners mingled, talking 'shop' and not much else.
Most of his fellow business associates were years
older than he was and he had little in common with
them, apart from a love of the land. In fact, he
would have rather avoided this particular gathering
altogether, if it wasn't for a small niggle deep in
his gut telling him that if he could get Sam alone,
away from work, she might open up to him.

So, he'd done it. Booked flights to Sydney,
rooms in one of the city's top hotels and tickets to
the conference and dinner, all in the hope that the
woman who piqued his interest more with each

passing day would come clean and divulge some small part of her life to him.

Despite many cunning attempts to drag any snippet of information from her, she'd held fast, not giving him one iota about herself. And the more she kept him guessing, the more intrigued he'd become, till he could hardly function these days without wondering what made Samantha Piper tick.

As for their physical attraction, he'd managed to keep his libido under control. Just. He'd grown used to cold showers at the end of a day's work, where he'd spent endless hours resisting the lure of her light, floral fragrance, the forbidden glimpse of cleavage as she reached across his desk or the tantalising sweep of her tongue as it moistened her lips while she concentrated on a particular task. Yes, it had been hell working with her these last few months and pretending he didn't feel anything for his luscious employee, but what else could he do?

He valued her astute opinions as a business-woman and didn't want to risk losing her, despite his reluctance to hire her in the first place. Sure, he'd toyed with their attraction on a few occasions but, thankfully, she'd put him back in his place. At least one of them had some semblance of self-control; otherwise, he could see their whole arrangement going up in flames, in more ways than one.

Knocking briskly at Sam's door, he wondered if she'd make any reference to their interlude on the plane. She hadn't mentioned the other kisses they'd shared, though a small part of him wished she would.

However, as she opened the door, Dylan didn't have time to ponder Sam's reasoning. Instead, all he could do was gape at the exquisite vision before him. Her body was wrapped in a soft blue fabric that hugged in all the right places and brought out the matching flecks in her green eyes. She'd used subtle make-up to highlight her features and had pinned her curls back in some sort of elaborate arrangement. Her overall appearance screamed 'grab me' and he had to curb the sudden impulse to do exactly that.

'Right on time. I like a man who's punctual.' Sam smiled, taking Dylan's gob-smacked look as an indication of approval. She twirled, revelling in the unique feel of chiffon swishing around her ankles. 'You like?'

He nodded, an expression of wonder lighting up his face and she had her answer. 'You look incredible,' he murmured, surveying her from head to foot.

Her skin tingled under the intensity of his stare and she resisted the impulse to rub her bare arms. 'Good. I know this dinner is important to you and I wanted to make an impression.'

He whistled, long and low. 'Well, you've certainly done that.'

She picked up her evening bag and pretended to swat him with it. 'Not on you, on your colleagues.'

'Who?' He continued to stare at her and she wondered if he'd lost his mind.

'Your colleagues. You know, those people you do business with, the same ones we're going to have dinner with.'

He shook his head. 'Change of plans. Room service. Here. Now.'

She laughed and tucked her hand through the crook of his arm. 'Thanks for the compliment. Now let's go.'

When Sam had purchased the dress she had known it looked good on her: the strapless bodice had highlighted her delicate shoulders, the fitted line accentuating her slim figure. However, though she'd craved Dylan's approval, she'd been totally unprepared for the blatant desire that blazed from his eyes when he'd first seen her and for one dizzying moment she thought he might take her into his arms, back her into the room and kick the door shut.

'How do you expect me to concentrate on business tonight with you looking like that?'

'Like what?' She smiled, enjoying her power as a woman, one who could hold the interest of a man like Dylan.

He waited till the doors of the lift slid shut before answering. 'Like every man's fantasy come to life.'

The smile slipped from her face as he placed both hands on her shoulders and bent towards her, his lips brushing hers. She'd been unprepared for the kiss, though she didn't stop to analyse it as she responded with matching eagerness, wrapping her arms around him and moulding against the lean hardness of his body. He kissed her like a man starved, a deep, endless kiss that reached down to her very soul and it affected her more than she wanted to admit. She didn't need this complication in her life, this overwhelming, helpless feeling that she belonged to him.

He groaned as she pulled away and buried her face into the crook of his neck. However, rather than calming her, his aftershave infused her senses

as she took a steadying breath and threatened to
tear apart what was left of her self-control.

'Hey, no use in hiding,' he whispered in her ear,
his lips raining a blazing trail of light kisses from
her earlobe to the hollow above her collarbone.

'Dylan—'

He silenced her with a quick peck on the lips.
'Let's not talk about this right now.'

As she opened her mouth to respond, he placed
a finger against it. 'Shh. Call it a momentary lapse
on my part.'

Sam didn't have time to speak as the doors of
the lift slid open and in walked the last man she
had expected, or wanted, to see.

CHAPTER EIGHT

'HELLO, Samantha. What are you doing here?'

If Dylan's scintillating kiss hadn't already un-
dermined Sam's confidence, the sight of Max
Sherpov staring down his aristocratic nose at her
would have.

She schooled her face into what she hoped was
a mask of nonchalance while her insides churned
with dread. 'Hi, Max. I'm here on business.'

'Oh?' Max raised an eyebrow and glanced at
Dylan, at her dress and back again.

Resisting the urge to tug at her bodice, she
squared her shoulders. 'Max, this is Dylan
Harmon.' She had known the instant Max had entered the lift that her cover was about to be blown
to kingdom come.

Dylan stuck out his hand. 'Pleased to meet you.'
Though by the expression on his face Sam knew
his words didn't ring true.

'Max is an old friend of the family,' she continued, wanting to fill the awkward silence that had
descended on them.

As the doors slid open on the ground floor Max

shook his head, the supercilious smirk that she despised marring his haughty features. 'Come now, Samantha, I'm much more than that.'

Staring at Max with all the disdain she could muster, she said, 'If you'll excuse us, Max, our table is waiting. Nice seeing you again.' She slipped a hand into Dylan's and strolled from the lift, hoping her jelly-like legs would hold her upright, at least till they reached the ballroom.

Thankfully, Dylan seemed just as anxious to escape Max's overbearing presence and gave her hand a reassuring squeeze as they were led to their table. He didn't speak till they were seated, giving her valuable time to compose herself. Seeing Max had shaken her more than she cared to admit. Or was it the fact that she would now have to answer questions that may have far-reaching consequences to her future with the man still holding her hand?

'Nice company you keep.'

'Hey, I don't pick my parents' friends.'

'Is that all he is to you?'

Sam resisted the urge to stick her fingers down her throat and make vomiting sounds at the thought of Max being anything but a friend to her. 'What do you think?'

Dylan relinquished her hand, leaving her strangely bereft. 'I think that old guy is smitten with you.' She barely heard his, 'Not that I blame him.'

She shrugged, hating herself for having to perpetuate the lie she'd woven. 'He means nothing to me. My parents seem to like him, which is more than I can say for me.'

'He acted as if he owned you,' Dylan persisted, gnawing away at her waning resistance. 'Especially that wisecrack about meaning more to you.'

Sam couldn't hold out much longer. She needed to tell Dylan some snippet of truth, otherwise he wouldn't stop till he'd dragged the whole sordid story from her. She sighed, wishing she hadn't started down the disastrous road that her harebrained scheme had managed to steer her. 'My parents seem to think that Max would make good husband material.'

'What?' Dylan exploded. 'But he's old enough to be your father!'

'Try telling that to my folks.' She could hardly believe that after all the years her parents had lived in Australia they hadn't lost any of their European heritage, hanging on to archaic traditions with grim determination.

'But why?'

Sam had to tread carefully here if she didn't want her whole lie to unravel before her eyes.

'They have old-fashioned values, believing that every woman needs a man to take care of her, to provide for her. A woman's place should be in the home, not the boardroom.'

She watched the shock register in his eyes and hoped that his interrogation would end sooner rather than later. 'Then why let you attend university? Why the degree?'

Sam shrugged, remembering the fateful day when she'd enrolled in the course and plucked up the courage to tell her parents. 'Simple, really. I blackmailed them.'

His eyebrows shot up. 'Tell me more.'

'I told them that if they didn't let me attend university I'd elope with David Peters.'

Dylan shook his head. 'I'm almost afraid to ask.' A hint of a smile tugged at the corners of his mouth. 'Who is David Peters?'

'My high school sweetheart. Not that he knew anything about it.' She chuckled at the memory of freckly, brace-face David, wondering what she'd ever seen in her dorky lab partner. 'I just used the idea of him to frighten my parents into giving in to me.'

'You're amazing, you know that?' He reached over and twisted a stray curl around his fingertip, the tenderness in his gaze causing her heart to flip-flop. 'Let's make a deal. For tonight, there will be no more talk of David, Max or any other men you have hidden in your past. Tonight, there's just you and me.'

Her breath hitched as he leaned towards her and for one crazy moment she thought he would kiss her, just like he had in the lift. Instead, he whispered in her ear, 'Does that sound like a plan to you?'

Sam could only nod as he planted a soft kiss near her temple before he pulled away to acknowledge the first of the other table occupants to arrive. However, as the evening proceeded and she endured the endless small talk, the boring speeches and picked at the food on her plate, she was constantly aware of the man at her side and his overwhelming presence. And, furthermore, what would happen once he walked her back to her room?

Would she have the willpower to refuse him if he kissed her again? Did she really want to? Though her experience with men was limited, she knew that a man like Dylan wouldn't be satisfied with a few snatched kisses for long. In responding to his kisses she'd probably given him the wrong idea and what if he demanded more?

Sneaking a quick peek at the man in question, she knew her body would have little trouble in overruling her head if he wrapped her in his arms and kissed her senseless.

But what about her heart?

Unfortunately, she'd already lost that particular organ to Dylan Harmon and he held it right where she didn't want it—in the palm of his hand.

Dylan repeatedly punched and pummelled his pillow, hoping the simple action might help him fall asleep. It didn't. He'd tossed and turned for the last hour, his head filled with images of the woman in the room next door, taunting him to follow through with what he'd started earlier.

Damn, he'd been a fool, allowing her to slip through his fingers when, right now, he could be having the best sex of his life with a woman who fired his passion with a simple flick of her shoulder-length hair.

As expected, the evening had bored him to tears, yet he'd been aware of Sam for every second of it. Having her by his side had filled him with pride, though for the life of him he couldn't fathom why. She was his employee yet he'd treated her like a cherished partner, a fact that hadn't gone unnoticed by the bulk of his associates. He'd be the talk of Sydney in the morning—the sooner he escaped back to Melbourne with Sam, the better. Or, better yet, he could whisk her away to Budgeree and finish what they'd started.

Why hadn't he pushed her harder? He'd walked her back to her room, his hand in the small of her back doing little for his restraint. The feel of her hot skin through the thin, gauzy material of her dress had beckoned him, urging him to do something completely out of character, like tear it off her. Instead, he'd stood outside her door, staring at her with what he'd hoped was a clear message in his eyes, not saying much at all.

And what had she done? Planted an all-too-brief kiss on his cheek, thanked him for an 'interesting' evening and closed her door, leaving him gawking like a jilted teenager. So much for sweeping her off her feet and into his bed. All he'd succeeded in doing was gaining another sleepless night, though not for the reason he'd anticipated.

Rolling out of bed, he padded across the dark room and pulled back the curtains, taking in the glittering view of Sydney laid out like a sparkling fairyland many storeys below. He'd always had a soft spot for this city though his heart belonged on the vast tracts of land in northern Victoria, where he could ride for miles in solitude and gaze upon the Harmon acreage with pride. Sam had seemed to instinctively understand his love of Budgeree, even though she didn't share his love of family responsibility. Not that he blamed her, after hearing about her parents' archaic views on marriage.

He unwittingly clenched his fists at the thought of her tied to that ancient crone Max. Hell, he'd wanted to pummel the man to death for the lecherous way he'd looked at Sam, not to mention the pitying glance the old man had sent his way, as if he didn't stand a chance.

Do you want a chance?

Turning away from the million-dollar view, he rubbed his temples and headed back to bed. Damned if he knew.

Sam silently cursed as she walked along the concourse towards the boarding gate, seeing but not quite believing her eyes. She'd never believed in coincidence or bad karma, yet how could she explain running into Quade in Melbourne, Max last night and now this, the unexpected appearance of two other men in her life? It had to be fate's way of paying her back for all the lies she'd told over the last few months.

'Hey, Princess. Fancy seeing you here.' Nick, her youngest brother, enveloped her in a bear hug.

'Yeah, Sis. You're looking good. What are you doing in Sydney?' Peter, the second oldest, tweaked her nose just as he'd always done. 'And where's the man?'

Sam prayed that Dylan would not appear in the next few minutes. He'd wanted to buy some obscure farming magazine and she hoped that the newsagency had to go through a backlog of stock to find it.

'He's around,' she said, keeping her answer purposely vague. 'What are you two doing here?'

A faint blush stained Peter's cheeks. Unfortunately, he possessed the same fair Popov complexion she did. 'Uh, I was invited to some fancy party and Nicky wanted to accompany me, to scope out the ladies.'

'Whose party?' Sam hid a grin, knowing exactly whose event Peter had flown down to Sydney to attend. He must be keener than she had thought, because he usually hated leaving the Brisbane sunshine and he hated flying even more.

'Ebony's parents threw some fancy shindig to raise money for disadvantaged kids, so I thought I'd lend a helping hand.' Peter paused and looked away, cementing Sam's suspicions that her brother was more smitten than he'd like to believe. 'I'm surprised you weren't there, showing off your betrothed.'

'Her *what*?'

Sam jumped, unaware that Dylan had walked up

behind her. Before she could answer, Nick thrust out his hand. 'You must be Dylan. Pleased to meet you. I'm Nick and this is Pete, brothers to this crazy woman.'

She slowly exhaled, unaware that she'd been holding her breath. If Nick had mentioned their surname she would have really had some explaining to do. Not that she was off the hook entirely.

Something akin to relief flashed across Dylan's face. 'Yes, I'm Dylan, though you guys obviously know more about me than I know about you.'

Peter rolled his eyes. 'Yeah, that'd be right. Keeping you in the dark, is she? That's our sis.'

Sam intervened quickly, wishing she could drag Dylan away before things turned really ugly. 'Why would I talk about you two when we've got more important things to discuss?' She threaded her arm through Dylan's and stared up at him, hoping to convince her brothers about the authenticity of her make-believe betrothal yet not wanting to alert Dylan to the fact.

Nick guffawed. 'I just bet you do.' He grabbed Peter's arm. 'Come on. Let's leave the two love-birds alone. Later, Princess. Dylan.'

As her brothers walked away, chuckling at some joke, Sam wished the floor would open up and swallow her whole.

'Lovebirds? Betrothed?' Dylan said quietly, disengaging from her grip. 'Where did your brothers get that idea? And why does everyone you know call you princess?'

This was it. Sink or swim time. Once again, she opted for the partial truth rather than a full-blown lie.

'You don't know my brothers. The five of them are a pain in the butt. They've always teased me, especially about boyfriends and stuff like that. I told them you were my boss, so it's their warped sense of humour to tease me in front of you. And I've already explained the marriage thing. If I spend more than two seconds in the company of any man, they nearly send out the wedding invites! Sick, huh?' She swallowed, needing to ease the dryness of her parched throat. She'd never been any good at telling lies but, with this much practice, she would soon be an expert. 'As for the princess thing, same reason. My brothers and their friends have always called me that, just because I hate it.'

Dylan stared at her face, as if trying to read every telltale line. Thankfully, the final boarding call for their flight boomed from the loudspeakers and she bent to pick up her hand luggage, breaking his intense scrutiny.

'You certainly have an interesting family.'

She breathed a sigh of relief, knowing he'd bought her concocted story and hating every minute of it. 'You call them interesting. I prefer wacky.'

He laid a restraining hand on her arm as she turned away. 'Don't underestimate the value of family. They're the most important thing in the world.'

Sam stiffened but didn't respond. She didn't need a lecture on family values from a man who wouldn't understand what she'd been through growing up; it had been difficult enough being a teenager without the added pressure of some obsolete royal title being bestowed on her like a prize she should treasure yet didn't want. Let him spout a whole lot of platitudes about family—as far as she was concerned, nothing he could ever say would change how she felt.

'Let's get back to Melbourne,' she said, knowing that the further away she got from the far-reaching influence of the Popovs, the better.

If Dylan had thought that meeting Sam's brothers might encourage her to open up to him more, he was wrong. Despite his attempts to draw her into conversation regarding the rest of her family, her childhood or anything remotely personal, she'd thwarted him at every turn, leaving him with the distinct impression that she had some deep, dark secret. And now, as her three-month trial period drew to a close, he was no nearer to knowing anything about the woman who had sneaked under his carefully erected barriers against emotional involvement.

He wanted to make her position as his personal assistant permanent. It would be the perfect solution, providing him with a valuable asset to his business life and giving him an opportunity to explore the unfamiliar, burgeoning feelings that she'd aroused within him. For he couldn't deny it any longer; despite her attempts to keep him at arm's length since their return from Sydney, he knew that he wanted her. He genuinely liked her yet wouldn't go as far as to admit to the other 'L' word.

He still couldn't acknowledge that word or the helpless feelings it reinforced—he'd lost his father because he'd been too pig-headed to admit to that emotion, yet he'd be damned if he associated 'love' and 'Sam' in the same thought.

So, that left him with only one option. Offer her a permanent position as his PA and see what developed between them. Luckily, he knew just the way to convince her to accept his offer.

CHAPTER NINE

AS SOON as they entered the gates to Budgeree a strange sense of belonging enveloped Sam again. She stared out the window, wishing she didn't feel this way. It would be hard enough walking away from Dylan next week without the added complication of yearning for a lifestyle she could never have. Not that she'd harboured any desire to live on the land before now—in fact, she'd been a city girl her entire life, eagerly escaping her family's acres in northern Queensland to live the high life in Brisbane. Though that probably had more to do with leaving the shackles of the Popovs behind rather than any burning desire to live in the city.

'You like this place, don't you?' Dylan spoke softly, as if reluctant to break the spell that seemed to envelop them the moment he'd pulled up in front of the homestead and switched off the engine.

She nodded. 'There's just something about it that reaches out and grabs you.'

He smiled, his warmth infusing her with some indefinable emotion that she dare not analyse. 'I'm glad you feel that way. It makes things a lot easier.'

Sam looked away quickly before she drowned in the endless depths of his dark eyes, not willing to ask him what he meant by 'things'. Instead, she flung open the car door and climbed out, wondering what had possessed her to accompany him on this trip. Sure, he'd badgered her into it, saying her presence was vital in finalising a few business contracts, but she hadn't been fooled. She'd noticed a certain gleam in Dylan's eye since they'd returned from Sydney, as if he wouldn't take no for an answer the next time they were alone together.

And sure enough, he'd made it perfectly clear that there would be no 'chaperon' at Budgeree this time, a fact that had made her pulse race in a potent mixture of anticipation and trepidation.

She followed him into the house, admiring the long, confident strides that spoke volumes about the man. Nothing intimidated him and he walked as if he owned the world, allowing nobody to stand in his way. Even in faded jeans and a casual shirt, he exuded an aura of power, one that seemed to draw her in deeper with each passing day.

'You can sleep in here…if you want.' He deposited her bag in the spare room she'd inhabited last time, though his significant pause left her in little doubt as to where he hoped she'd be sleeping, or *not* sleeping, tonight.

'Thanks.' She strode across the room, pulled back the curtains and took in the stunning view, needing to focus on something, anything, other than Dylan. He seemed to dwarf everything in the room and the longer he stood there, staring at her with those enigmatic eyes, the harder it would be to maintain a platonic distance.

Hoping he'd take the hint that she wanted to be alone, Sam continued to stare out the window.

'Is everything all right?'

She jumped, wishing she hadn't turned her back on him. Rather than leaving the room, he'd sneaked up behind her, his voice a mere whisper away from her ear.

'I'm fine,' she said, moving away from the welcoming heat radiating off his body in waves.

'No, you're not.' He reached out and snagged her arm, stopping her in her tracks. 'Tell me what's wrong.'

She stared at his hand, wishing she could shake it off, pick up her bag and high tail it out of this house and out of his life. Who had she been kidding? She could no more resist this man than denounce her heritage—and the sooner she faced facts, the better.

'Maybe later.' She pulled away and, thankfully, he released her. She unzipped her bag and started fumbling with her clothes, furiously blinking away the tears that had inexplicably filled her eyes. She'd never been prone to tears, yet the way her emotions had been swinging lately, she'd been close to waterworks several times.

'I'm here for you, Samantha.' His low voice reached out and wrapped her in comforting warmth, beckoning her to turn around, bury her head against his chest and sob out her sorry tale.

Instead, she nodded, not trusting herself to speak as the tears trickled down her cheeks. Thankfully, he didn't touch her and only hesitated a moment longer before leaving the room. As soon as she heard the latch click, she sank on to the bed, buried her face in her hands and cried, though for the life of her she couldn't figure out if they were tears of regret for her soon-to-be departure, shame at her lies, or the fact that she was about to lose the man she'd been foolish enough to fall in love with.

Dylan had no idea why Sam had appeared so upset when they'd first arrived earlier that afternoon, though her strange behaviour had certainly put a dent in his plans. He'd had it all figured out—lay out a lavish dinner, ply her with fine wine, then offer her the job of a lifetime. And if anything else developed… Well, he'd managed to rein in his imagination before his libido took off at a gallop.

Now, he didn't know whether he should wait till tomorrow and try again or repack the four-wheel drive, throw in the towel and head back to Melbourne. Maybe he'd misread the signals and Sam wasn't interested in him after all? Perhaps she'd responded to his kisses out of some warped sense of duty for her boss rather than any real feeling? And maybe, just maybe, he'd been foolish enough to depend on this woman too much and couldn't bear the thought of losing her and that was why he was hell-bent on her accepting this job.

Dylan was no fool. He knew there would be other personal assistants just as competent as Sam, yet he was driven to make her accept his offer in the vain hope they could explore their developing feelings.

Correction. *His* developing feelings.

He grimaced, wondering when he'd become such a sucker. He'd managed to stay single and emotionally tangle-free for the last few years, just the way he liked it. Yet here he was, already pining for a pint-sized blonde dynamo who would probably walk out of his life in a week without a backward glance, taking her damn secrets with her.

'Women,' he muttered under his breath, slamming the back door as he headed for the stables. A fast and furious ride was in order, anything to get the adrenaline flowing and to rid himself of this emotional lethargy that seemed to be sapping him of every ounce of common sense he possessed.

And if Sam wanted anything more from him other than a pay cheque before the end of next week, she would just have to show him.

Sam dug her heels into the mare's sides, urging her to follow the distant streak across the horizon at any pace faster than a slow trot. She'd ridden Speedy last time, soon recognising that the plodding mare had been named in the typical Australian way of labelling opposite characteristics: Bluey for redheads, Shorty for anyone over six feet tall and Mouse for the powerful stallion that Dylan now rode like a man possessed.

True to form, Speedy could barely raise a canter as she followed her stable-mate and Sam resigned herself to the fact that she'd eventually catch up with Dylan and his mount—some time tomorrow!

She'd seen him tear out of the stable, driving his horse like a madman with a million demons on his tail. Strangely enough, she'd wanted to take a ride this afternoon in the hope it might clear her head and it seemed Dylan had the same idea. Though she'd hardly call his hair-raising gallop a leisurely ride.

So she'd followed him, not wanting to lose her way on the vast plains of Budgeree and hoping that she'd know what to say the next time she saw him. Though the tears she'd shed earlier had been cathartic, she still had no idea how she could bear to leave Dylan next week. She had an inkling he might ask her to stay on in the position of PA but what would that achieve, apart from prolonging the agony?

Besides, her parents wouldn't wait too much longer to meet her 'betrothed' and she didn't want her elaborate lie falling down around her ears, with Dylan witnessing it. She'd had enough close calls as it was and couldn't believe that her luck had held out this far. No, she only had one choice and that was to leave next week as planned and return to her family, in the hope they would now accept the undeniable proof that she could make it on her own without the support of any man as her husband and chief protector. And, hopefully, Dylan would be none the wiser to his involvement in her plan or the fact that she'd lost her heart to him.

As if on cue, his vision rose before her, man and stallion standing still on a ridge, silhouetted against the vibrant ochre setting sun. Sam swallowed the lump of emotion that had risen in her throat, wishing she could imprint this moment on her mind for ever, a cherished memory she could resurrect at will during the lonely months ahead.

Dylan turned as if sensing her presence and guided Mouse down the hill towards her. She waited for him, suddenly overcome by a powerful desire that this could be a life she could get used to; riding out to meet the man of her dreams at the end of every day and accompanying him home, to their home, where they could stay wrapped in each other's arms all night and face whatever the next day would bring, together.

Sam resisted the urge to shake her head and dislodge the ridiculous fantasy that had popped into her mind. There would be no shared life at Budgeree, no welcoming homecomings, no man of her dreams. Instead, she would be left with nothing...apart from the chance to make the most of every second she had left with the man she loved. Once the idea insinuated its way into her head, she couldn't ignore it. What harm could it do, to make the most of their remaining time together? Treasured memories would be the only thing left to sustain her in the months ahead, when the full force of what she'd really lost would hit her.

Squaring her shoulders as he stopped beside her,

she smiled. 'Thought you might get lost out here on your own.'

His frown softened as he reached towards her and ran an index finger lightly down her cheek. 'You had a smudge of dirt there.' He straightened up quickly, depriving her of the chance to lean against his hand. 'You shouldn't have followed me out here. I don't have time to send out a search party if you'd got lost.'

Sam noted his rigid posture and the frown that hadn't quite disappeared yet. If she was going to make him want her tonight, she had her work cut out for her. 'I had no choice. When Speedy wants her man, she'll stop at nothing. I just sat along for the ride.'

His eyes darkened imperceptibly in the waning light and she resisted the urge to squirm in the saddle. 'Yeah, well, some females are like that.'

Silence stretched between them as she struggled to find something bright and witty to say. Thankfully, Mouse pawed the ground as if keen to get moving, breaking their deadlocked·stare.

'Let's head back. I'm starving.' He wheeled around, not sending her a backward look.

So am I, Dylan.

Though Sam knew her hunger had nothing to do with food and everything to do with the man sitting proudly on his horse, surveying his land. She'd made a lightning-fast decision several minutes ago and she hoped she now had the guts to go through with it. If this was her last week with Dylan, she would make the most of it, no tears, no regrets. She wanted him, more than she'd ever wanted any man in her entire life and, for tonight, she would cast aside her inhibitions, her common sense and every self-preservation mechanism that screamed she was doing the wrong thing, and go after him. No holds barred.

She smiled as the homestead came into sight, knowing that Dylan wouldn't know what hit him when she pulled out all stops tonight. And prayed she'd have the strength to walk away when it was all over.

Dylan sat in the worn recliner that had been his dad's favourite and stretched his legs out towards the blazing fire.

'Here's your port. Cheers.' Sam touched the rim of her glass to his before raising it to her lips and taking a sip.

He gulped, wishing he could tear his gaze away from her mouth while simultaneously wishing for those lips to do a whole lot more.

'Cheers,' he murmured, knowing that for as long

as he lived he would never figure women out.
Since their ride, Sam had done her best to appear
cheerful and relaxed, the exact opposite of her de-
meanour when they'd arrived.

She'd made small talk over dinner and had appeared genuinely interested in his plans for this
place, his pride and joy. He hadn't felt so comfortable in a woman's presence in a long time and
knew that now was as good a time as any to broach
the subject of her ongoing contract.

'Samantha, we need to talk.'

To his amazement, she laughed and reached for
his glass. 'Are you ever going to lighten up and
call me Sam?'

He could've sworn she sashayed across the
room, setting their glasses on the mantelpiece before turning to face him, an inviting little smile
playing across her lips. 'Well?'

He leaned back in the chair and placed his hands
behind his head, admiring her silhouette with the
fire at her back. In response, she stretched her arms
back towards the heat and rubbed her hands together, the simple action pulling her shirt taut
against her chest and outlining the curve of her
breasts.

Heat surged through his body as he fought the
impulse to drag her down to the sheepskin rug in

front of the fire and tear open her shirt. 'So, you think I need to lighten up?'

'I know you do.' As if reading his mind, she sank on to the rug and he almost salivated as his fantasy took flight. He imagined peeling the clothes from her body, exposing the exquisite flesh beneath to his hands…

'Dylan?' Even the soft, breathy way she uttered his name had him focusing on all the wrong cues. If he didn't know any better, he could've sworn she wanted him as much as he wanted her.

He practically leaped from the chair and strode towards the door before he did something really dumb, like join her on that damn rug. 'I'm going to bed. See you in the morning.'

'Mind if I join you?'

Her whisper stopped him dead in his tracks.

'What did you just say?' He turned, knowing his fantasy must've turned into an auditory hallucination yet wishing against hope that he'd just heard correctly.

She didn't respond immediately and he knew he must be going mad. However, just as he was about to walk out the door, she held out her hand to him. 'Come here, Dylan.'

He crossed the room in an instant, sank to his

knees in front of the crackling fire and pulled her into his arms.

'Well, don't just sit there. Aren't you going to kiss me?'

Dylan didn't need further encouragement as he bent his head and covered her mouth in a searing kiss. She moaned and he lost all sense of control, plundering her mouth with the abandon of a man starved and pulling her flush against him, sealing their bodies together, needing to feel her pressed against him.

Rather than stopping him, which his dazed mind half expected her to do, she melded into him, her hands clamping around his neck and hanging on for dear life. She stroked the nape of his neck, her fingernails lightly grazing his skin while her mouth nibbled hot kisses across his jaw. Sparks flew— and not just from the sap of a log that suddenly ignited in the hearth.

In a strangled voice he managed to ask, 'Are you sure about this?'

'No more questions,' she whispered against the side of his mouth. 'Tonight is about you and me. Think you can handle it?'

Before he could answer, she pulled him towards her for another kiss and they sank into the downy softness of the rug. He claimed her lips, feasting on the sweetness of liquor and pure Sam.

'I want you, Sam,' he murmured, as he undid each button on her shirt before sliding his hand beneath the scrap of lace that encased her breasts, his fingers stroking the soft skin till he thought he'd lose his mind.

Sam arched towards Dylan as his thumb grazed her nipple, shards of electrifying fire shooting through her body. She'd lost control the minute he'd first touched her…and she was loving every minute of it.

'You pick a fine time to finally call me Sam,' she managed to gasp out as his fingers momentarily left her breast and splayed across her stomach before moving lower, creating an instant yearning that wouldn't be satisfied with anything less than his naked body joined with hers. The passion between them left her more than a little scared. In fact, right now, with his hands skating over her skin with skilled precision, she was downright terrified.

'Timing is everything, sweetheart.' He gathered her to him and cradled her, as if sensing her sudden panic.

She stared at the man she loved in the flickering firelight, wondering if the tenderness she glimpsed in his eyes was a figment of her overheated imagination.

'Trust me,' he whispered, brushing a wayward curl back from her face before tracing a slow, deliberate line from her temple to her lips, his finger skimming over her bottom lip repeatedly, firing her need with each gentle stroke.

She barely managed a nod as he rose, holding her in his arms and walked through the old homestead towards the master bedroom.

Sam woke to the raucous chuckles of a kookaburra and stretched, wondering what had happened to her cotton T-shirt during the night. She always wore the faded rugby shirt to bed yet it had miraculously disappeared. Suddenly, she sat bolt upright, clutched the sheet to her breasts and glanced around the room as memories of last night flooded back.

So, it hadn't been a dream.

She was in the master bedroom, with its antique Blackwood furniture and burgundy lined curtains, lying in the king-sized four-poster bed, wearing nothing but a smile. And the man who had put it there was nowhere in sight.

She'd been dreading this moment ever since she'd thrown caution to the wind yesterday and decided to make love with Dylan. How should she act afterwards? What should she say? After all, they weren't strangers who could walk away without a backward glance. She still had a job to do, even if it was only for another week. Yet how could she face him now, with the scorching memories of their lovemaking burned into her brain, and keep their relationship strictly platonic?

Determined not to make a fool of herself, she slid out of bed and winced, aching in muscles she didn't know existed. She needed a shower, fresh clothes and a steaming mug of coffee in that order. Then, and only then, could she entertain the thought of facing Dylan.

Picking up her discarded clothes from the floor, she crept across the hallway and scurried into her room, thankful that the man who had rocked her world last night was nowhere in sight. Maybe she'd figure out what to say during her shower? She should probably keep their initial conversation light, something like 'the overtime in this job is a killer.' Yeah, right, then he'd think she was a total loser.

She sighed with pleasure as she stepped into the steaming shower and let the hot water sluice down her body, wondering if he was avoiding her. Not that she could blame him—he probably thought she'd lost her marbles, coming on to him last night after practically falling apart earlier that afternoon.

No doubt about it. She would have a lot of explaining to do... If she ever plucked up enough courage to leave the shelter of her room.

Reaching for the soap, her hand stilled as a blast of cold air hit her back, closely followed by the enveloping warmth of a hard, male body. An *aroused*, male body, pressing firmly against her.

'Let me do that.' Dylan wrapped his arms around her from behind and she leaned back, her legs turning to jelly as he soaped the front of her body, circling her breasts in slow, concentric circles till she groaned aloud.

So much for figuring out what to say to him. There wasn't much need for talking as she lost herself in Dylan.

As her heart rate returned to a pace resembling normal, she sagged against him, not trusting herself to speak.

'See you in the kitchen. We've got work to do.' He planted a quick peck under her earlobe and stepped out of the shower, as if the last twenty-four hours had never happened.

And, just like that, Sam realised that the secret dream she'd been harbouring for the last few months, the one where Dylan would fall madly in love with her and really become her fiancé, had been just that, a fanciful dream.

Now, it was time to wake up.

CHAPTER TEN

SAM deserved an Oscar. In fact, she deserved a whole truckload of acting awards for the performance she'd put on today. She'd been the epitome of the efficient PA, just as her boss wanted. For that's how Dylan had behaved all day, like a tyrannical boss who demanded nothing less than perfection from an employee. There hadn't been a hint of the intimacies they'd shared last night, not to mention their steamy session in the shower this morning.

Instead, he'd pretended nothing had happened between them and she'd picked up on his cues and followed suit. After all, it was for the best. They had no future beyond next week and it was time she started to believe it.

'Could you pass me that document?' Dylan gestured towards the pile of papers to her left while studying the invoice in his hand.

'So much for the magical P word,' she muttered, resisting the urge to throw the paper at him.

'Don't be childish.' He glared at her as if she'd uttered some obscenity.

She quirked an eyebrow. 'Since when are manners considered childish?'

He ignored her and returned to studying the document, while her temper rose several notches. She'd tolerated his barked commands and surly attitude all day, knowing there was only so much she could take. Though he'd been demanding over the past few months, he'd never been rude and she wondered if his churlish display today was designed to push her away. If so, he was doing a fine job of it.

She took a calming breath and returned to adding the column of figures she'd been working on, wishing her own life was as easy to compute.

'By the way, we're leaving as soon as we've finished this pile.'

She looked up in time to find him staring at her with an odd expression on his face before he quickly returned to the paper in his hand.

'Thanks for the notice,' she said, wondering what had happened to the easy-going camaraderie they'd shared before last night. Rather than bringing them closer as she'd anticipated, their interlude had widened the gap between them to unbreachable proportions.

'I'm not in the mood, Samantha.'

That did it. She'd had enough of his condescending tone and all-round bad attitude for one day. Standing up, she slammed the completed spreadsheet on the table in front of him and walked towards the door, only pausing when she reached it. 'Pity you didn't say the same last night. Would've saved us your little performance today.'

Shock spread across his face though she didn't give him a chance to reply. 'I'll meet you out the front in fifteen minutes,' she said, hoping her voice wouldn't quaver. 'After all, our *business* here is finished.'

She walked away, head held high, while for the second time in as many days Sam fought a useless battle against tears as she silently cursed the man who had turned her world upside down.

On their return to Melbourne, Dylan stalked into his room and flung his bag on to the floor, wondering how he'd managed to make such a mess of things. Rather than a sojourn at Budgeree opening the door to a deeper relationship with Sam, the time they'd spent there had well and truly slammed it shut. He'd acted like a jerk today, saying the wrong things and behaving like an ass, when what he'd really felt like doing was dragging her back to his bed and making wild, passionate love to her all day long.

And what had he done about it? Pushed her away in the coldest way possible, not daring to believe that he'd been foolish enough to fall in love with her. He didn't have room in his life for love. It was a useless emotion that complicated simple relationships and turned them into dependent affairs fraught with responsibilities. If anyone should know, he should. Just look at what had happened with his dad.

A knock interrupted his thoughts. 'Can I come in, Son?'

'Sure, Mum.' He took a deep breath, hoping she couldn't read the dejection on his face.

He should've known better. As soon as she entered the room, his mother honed in on his mood immediately. 'Is everything all right, love?'

'Of course.' He avoided eye contact, knowing he was a lousy liar when it came to the most important woman in his life. Pity he hadn't felt the same about his mum's competition earlier that day; after all, he'd had little trouble in hiding the truth about his feelings from Sam.

She sat down on his bed and patted the spot next to her. 'Come here and tell me all about it.'

He stiffened, not willing to admit the truth to his mum. Hell, he was having a hard enough time admitting it to himself.

And then, with the unerring precision of a lifetime spent reading her son, she honed in on the main problem. 'You're in love with her, aren't you?'

He schooled his face into an impassive mask, knowing it wouldn't fool his mum. 'You've been reading too many of those romance novels. Isn't it time you branched out into another genre, like crime?'

His mother shook her head, as if he'd disappointed her in some way. 'The only crime around here is the one occurring right in front of me. When are you going to learn that taking a chance on love isn't so bad?'

'Who said anything about love?'

She smiled, that same knowing smile she'd given him when he'd pulled out his first tooth and said that it had fallen out, when he'd fibbed about a stomach-ache to avoid an exam at school, when he'd said his first love bite was a result of a snooker cue accidentally hitting him in the neck. 'You don't have to say a thing. It's written all over your face.' She clasped her hands together as her grin broadened. 'A mother knows these things.'

'Leave it alone, Mum. I don't want to talk about it.' He paced the room, feeling like a circus lion about to be prodded into jumping through hoops.

'Well, if you don't want to talk to me, why don't you talk to the lady in question?'

An image of Sam's face as she'd flung that comment about his mood back at him before leaving Budgeree rose before his eyes; though she'd tried using sass to cover her hurt, he'd seen right through it, feeling like a real bastard in the process. And what had he done about it? Absolutely nothing.

'Sam and I need to sort out a few issues.' His mum's face brightened at his admission and he quickly held up a hand before she rushed out to start planning the wedding. 'They involve her ongoing employment, not the state of her heart. Or mine, for that matter.'

'Oh.'

He wondered at his mother's disappointment and why she'd grown to like Sam so much. Sure, she wanted to see him married off; after all, she'd been not-so-subtle in shoving him in Monique Taylor's direction for years, but why push him towards Sam? His mum had always been a bit of a prude when it came to mixing business with pleasure, hinting on several occasions that it was improper for him to flirt with the hired help.

Yet here she was, almost forcing him to admit his love for Sam. Why?

'Fine. If you want to talk to your decrepit old mother, I'm here for you.' She stood up and straightened her skirt. 'Just remember, darling. Follow your heart.' She kissed him on the cheek, leaving him alone with a host of unwelcome thoughts, most of them centred around Sam and how he could possibly make up to her for his atrocious behaviour.

Sam didn't bother unpacking on her return to Melbourne. Why bother, when she'd have to repack in a week? Or less, if she had her way. After all, why prolong the agony? Dylan had made it more than clear that he couldn't tolerate her presence in his life any longer and, after the way he'd behaved today, the feeling was entirely mutual.

Ebony had been right—love was for suckers. Though, by the goofy look on her brother Pete's face when he had mentioned her friend at the airport in Sydney, Ebony could be heading for a big fall—if she hadn't fallen all ready.

Tears sprang to Sam's eyes as she thought about her friend. She really needed a shoulder to cry on at the moment and Ebony would be perfect. Wiping her eyes with an angry swipe of her hand and cursing her stupidity at shedding tears for a man who definitely wasn't worth it, she made her way to the study, scanning the hall for the man she didn't want to bump into. A quick phone call to her friend would do wonders for her state of mind; if anyone could talk sense into her, Ebony could.

She punched out the number with impatient jabs of her index finger and held her breath while the phone rang. Thankfully, Ebony picked up on the fifth ring.

'Eb, it's me.'

'Hi, Sam. What's up? You sound awful.'

Sam sighed. 'That obvious, huh?'

'Oh-oh. What's he done?' Ebony always had the unerring talent of honing right in on a problem. It had annoyed Sam at times but, right now, she was grateful for it.

And, just like that, Sam poured out the whole sorry story to her best friend, leaving nothing out.

Ebony paused as Sam's tirade finished. 'Why don't you tell him the truth?'

Sam laughed, a bitter sound far from happiness. 'And say what? "Hey, Dylan, even though I've been your employee for the last three months, it's all been a lie and what I really want is for us to get married and live happily ever after." Yeah, right. I'm sure he'd love that.'

'I meant tell him the truth about how you feel. What have you got to lose?'

At that moment Sam heard a faint click behind her. She cupped a hand over the receiver and turned around, the sight of Dylan glowering at her sending her heart plummeting.

'We need to talk. Now.'

If she thought he'd been angry earlier, she'd underestimated him. The low, clipped tone he'd just used, along with the folded arms and fierce frown, indicated he'd surpassed anger and had entered the furious stage.

'I'll call you back later,' she said softly into the phone, swallowing to dislodge the lump of emotion that had risen in her throat.

'If that's who I think it is, go for it.' Another of Ebony's mottoes for life. Though, in this case, Sam knew it was way too late to follow her friend's advice. She'd already 'gone for it' and it had landed her in more trouble than it'd been worth.

'Bye.' As Sam replaced the receiver she wondered how much of her conversation Dylan had overheard. By the deepening frown and the way he stalked across the room towards her, he'd probably heard plenty.

'Sit down,' he snapped, pointing to the ergonomic chair she'd occupied almost every day over the last few months. 'And let's talk about your *employment*.'

'Don't make it sound so appealing,' she muttered, before quickly taking a seat. Though she didn't take kindly to being ordered around, she sensed that now was not the time to push the issue. Dylan looked mad as hell—and she'd been the one stupid enough to provoke him.

He clenched his fists and took several deep breaths before continuing. 'I actually came down here to offer you a permanent position as my PA. You've done a great job, better than I could've hoped for, and I thought it's time to cement our business arrangement.'

Sam didn't know what to say. She thought he'd overheard her conversation with Ebony and would subject her to an interrogation; instead, she almost sagged with relief as she realised he'd come down here to discuss her job. The angry mood was probably a carry-over from this morning—he hadn't spoken a word on their return trip to Melbourne, which had been fine with her. As she opened her mouth to respond, he held up a hand.

'Don't.'

He spat the word out and she knew in an instant that her relief had been short-lived.

'I don't want to hear another word out of your lying little mouth.' He stared at her, his eyes turning to molten chocolate as they smouldered with rage.

The little flicker of hope within Sam shrivelled and died as she realised he'd probably heard every damning word she'd just uttered on the phone. And she'd now have to come clean to the last man on earth she'd hoped would ever learn the truth.

'Let me explain—'

'I don't want to hear it,' he interrupted.

Sam sank further into the chair, wishing she could say something, anything, to allay the way he must be feeling right now. She hated being lied to, almost as much as she hated being pushed around by others, and she knew that Dylan wouldn't be satisfied with anything less than the truth.

However, before she could speak, he swung to face her again, neck muscles standing rigid against the collar of his shirt, an angry flush staining his tanned cheeks. 'I thought you were different, yet you're not. You're just like the rest. And I despise you for it.'

He'd startled her when he'd looked at her and her pulse had raced. Now, with icy contempt dripping from every word and his cold stare, the blood flowing in her veins froze.

'The rest?' She spoke quietly, hoping her tone would soothe him. It didn't.

'You lied to me, Samantha, just like the rest. I heard you admit it to whoever you were speaking to on the phone. You came here under the pretence of working for me, when all you really wanted was a ring on your finger and an easy way into the Harmon fortune. Well, forget it. Your little scheme hasn't worked. Now get out!'

Sam paled as Dylan fixed her with a stare that would have sent most of the men in his business world scuttling for cover. She didn't refute his accusations or offer any kind of explanation. Instead, she just sat there, clasping her hands together and shaking her head.

Pain, swift and raw, knifed his heart as he watched her, wishing she could have been different and knowing the wish was futile. He'd heard her say that her stint here had been a sham and what she'd hoped for was marriage.

So much for his instincts to read people. He'd been so careful in the past, not falling victim to the women who had entered his life with sweet, empty words designed to entice him. They hadn't loved him; instead, they'd all been out for one thing—an easy entry into the Harmon fortune. He'd managed to harden his heart and thwart them all. Until now.

However, all wasn't lost. He'd discovered Sam's

plan in time to save the family fortune, if not his heart.

He squared his shoulders and glared at her, instilling every ounce of hurt and betrayal into his voice. 'I said, get out!'

She stood and headed towards the door, not even casting a glance in his direction.

Dylan's heart shattered as he watched the woman he loved walk out of his life.

CHAPTER ELEVEN

'It's for the best…it's for the best…' Sam silently repeated the words over and over during the flight to Brisbane. However, as much as she tried to believe them, she couldn't ignore the image that seemed burned into her retinas, of Dylan's horrified expression as he'd flung accusations at her, hatred etched into every line of his face.

She should be angry. She should hate him for jumping to conclusions. Instead, she felt bereft, as if someone had reached into her chest and ripped her heart out. She'd never experienced such total and utter desolation and knew it would take a lifetime to recover from loving Dylan.

So what if her plan to prove her independence to her parents had succeeded? It would be a hollow victory, considering she'd lost her heart in the process.

Maybe she was just a tad mad at him for lumping her in with the rest of the bimbos who had tried to ensnare him, though she couldn't really blame him for adding two and two and coming up with five. He *had* overheard her say to Ebony she'd lied to him and, though she couldn't quite recall it, she'd mumbled something about marrying him too. Funnily enough, that little accusation hadn't been far from the truth. She would've married him in a second if he'd asked.

As the plane touched down and Sam disembarked, she scanned the crowd for her brother, Pete. Despite her protestations to Ebony that everything was all right when she'd called her from Melbourne airport, her friend had sensed trouble and insisted that she would notify Pete to pick her up when Sam arrived home. In no mood to argue at the time, Sam had reluctantly agreed. However, as Pete spotted her amongst the passengers and enveloped her in a bear hug, she wondered at her sanity. She was in no mood for lengthy interrogations or explanations, two things her brothers were experts at.

Stifling the urge to sob into Pete's shirt, Sam pulled away. 'Thanks for picking me up.'

'No problem.' Pete picked up her luggage and headed for the nearest exit, leaving Sam gaping.

'What? No questions? No prying?'

He stopped and turned around. 'Come on, Sis. It's me you're talking to.'

'That's what I'm afraid of. Since when did you become sensitive to my feelings?' Her brothers had taken it in turns to tease, berate and lecture her for most of her twenty-five years and she couldn't believe that Pete had turned over a new leaf now.

He shrugged, appearing strangely uncomfortable. 'I had a chat with Eb. She told me to lay off you, in no uncertain terms.'

Sam tried to smother a grin and failed. If she'd had any doubts about the blossoming relationship between Pete and her best friend, her brother had just laid them to rest. He must be head over heels to take advice from a woman, especially one as opinionated as Ebony.

'So, when's the wedding?' She couldn't resist teasing him, for it took the focus off her own problems for more than two seconds.

To her amazement, Pete blushed. 'She told you, didn't she?'

'Told me what?'

He shook his head. 'It's supposed to be a secret. Damn woman.'

Sam grabbed Pete's arm as a smidgeon of an idea took root and quickly grew to beanstalk proportions. '*You're* getting married?'

'Shh.' He glanced around as if she'd just announced it over the airport loudspeaker. 'Nobody knows and I'd like to keep it that way.'

'*You're* marrying *Ebony*?' Sam needed to find

the nearest chair—and fast—before she collapsed. 'You're kidding, right?'

Pete stared at her and she'd never seen her brother so serious. 'No, I'm not. We love each other, probably have for years, and it's time to make it official.'

'But why all the secrecy?'

'You of all people should know the answer to that one, Princess.'

And suddenly, with a blinding flash of clarity, Sam understood. While she'd been away, perhaps her brothers had borne some of her parents' pressure in 'holding up the Popov name' and 'marrying to fit their heritage'. At last, after all she'd had to endure over the last few years, she finally had an ally.

She leaned over and hugged Pete. 'I'm really happy for you. And, don't worry, your secret's safe with me. Though I'm going to kill Ebony. She didn't tell me a word.'

Pete squeezed her back. 'She didn't think it was the right time, what with your…um, situation…' He trailed off, as if he'd said too much.

Sam pasted a bright smile on her face, determined not to let her pain resurface in front of her brother. 'Hey, don't worry about me. I'll be fine.'

However, as he filled her in on the family news
as they travelled home, Sam seriously wondered if
she'd ever be fine again.

Dylan rarely drank, believing it impeded his judgement. However, as he downed a second straight
whiskey in the space of an hour, he allowed himself the luxury of a wry smile. He hadn't needed
alcohol to impede his judgement when it came to
Sam—he'd done a damn good job of botching it
all on his own.

Even now, after brooding on how foolish he'd
been to fall for her little act, he couldn't believe
that it was over. He dropped his head in his hands
and rubbed his temples, wishing the hot blonde
with the rapier mind and sharper wit had never
entered his life three months ago. He'd been behaving out of character ever since and, despite her
betrayal, a small part of him still wanted her more
than he'd ever wanted any woman.

'Why did Sam leave?'

His head snapped up at the sound of his
mother's voice. She must have sneaked into the
study, just as he had several hours earlier, though
what he'd overheard had changed his life for ever.

'She lied to me, Mum.'

His mother pulled up the nearest seat. 'So, she
told you, huh?'

'You *knew* about this?' He shook his head, hearing but not quite believing his own mother would support such a scheme. She would obviously go to any lengths to see him married off and it sickened him, almost as much as Sam's betrayal.

His mother shrugged, as if supporting a gold-digger and her claims to lay a hand on the Harmon fortune was no big deal. 'Yes, I knew. I guessed the truth when I first saw her and we had a little chat that confirmed it.'

Dylan took a deep breath, struggling to get air into his constricting lungs. 'And you supported her?'

'Well, she explained things to me and I didn't see any harm in it.'

He leaped up from his chair, his temper flaring out of control for the second time that day. 'You didn't see the harm in that little schemer setting her sights on using me to get at our fortune?' His voice rose several octaves. 'What were you thinking, Mum?'

To his amazement, his mother laughed. Not just an intimidated titter or a smothered chuckle, but an all-out belly laugh. 'Where did you get the idea that Sam was after our fortune?'

He folded his arms and glared at the one woman in the world he thought he could trust. 'I overheard her on the phone to someone earlier. She said she'd lied to me all this time and that she wanted to marry me.'

'Oh, dear.' His mother wiped away the tears from the corners of her eyes. 'You've got it all wrong, dear.'

'Have I?'

His mother nodded and, by the grave expression on her face, he suddenly knew he wouldn't like what he was about to hear. 'Have you heard of the Popov family?'

'Of course. Who hasn't? They own most of Queensland.'

'Did you also know they are descendants of Russian royalty?'

Dylan couldn't fathom where all this was leading but he decided to give his mother the benefit of the doubt. She rarely minced words and was obviously leading somewhere with all this. 'Get to the point, Mum.'

She reached for a handkerchief and dabbed at her nose. 'I don't think Sam was after the Harmon fortune. She wouldn't need it. She's a princess, Dylan.'

'*What?*' He'd never thought that age had affected his mum but maybe senility had crept up on her overnight?

'Samantha is the only daughter of the Popov family. And a rich princess in her own right.' His mum had the grace to look away, not quite able to meet his eye.

He managed a laugh, a strange bitter sound that echoed in the large room. 'I don't understand. Why the ruse? Why change her surname, why work for me, why mention marriage?' He shook his head, trying to make sense of the barrage of questions that swirled around his brain.

'Why don't you ask *her*?' His mother stood up and laid a comforting hand on his shoulder. 'It's the only way, Son.'

He stared at his mother's retreating back before reaching for the phone.

Sam's reunion with her parents hadn't gone quite as expected. She'd anticipated an interrogation of mammoth proportions, mainly revolving around her absent fiancé. Instead, they'd welcomed her with open arms, lavishing her with more love than they had in her twenty-five years to date. Rather than plying her with questions, they'd smothered her with emotion, reinforcing how much they'd missed her.

She couldn't handle this drastic change in her strict, orthodox parents and the truth had spilled out before she could stop it. Well, most of the truth.

She told them about working for Dylan Harmon to prove her independence, about the liberated feeling of living away from her family, about how Max actually made her skin crawl and the thought of marrying him would drive her away permanently. She'd cried tears of relief when they embraced her and apologised for driving her to such lengths, admitting that they hadn't realised the pressure they'd been placing on her and the rest of their children. The experience had been a catalyst in changing her relationship with her parents and, if she'd known what her harebrained scheme would do, she would have done it a long time ago.

She'd told them almost everything—leaving out the part where she'd lost her heart to a man who now despised her.

However, she hadn't had time to dwell on that. Once Pete had seen his parents' change of attitude, he'd told them about marrying Ebony and the entire family had been coerced into making the wedding happen as soon as possible. It had barely been a week since she'd returned from Melbourne and today her best friend would become her sister-in-law.

Putting the finishing touches to her make-up, she

knocked on the interconnecting door of the hotel room that the girls had hired to get ready for the big day. 'Are you finished, Eb? It's almost time to go.'

The door swung open and, in typical flamboyant style, her friend struck a pose. 'What do you think? Do I look like a bride?'

Sam smiled and brushed away the tears that sprang to her eyes at the sight of her friend clad in an ivory sheath dotted with crystals, her usually flyaway hair smoothed into a sleek chignon and adorned with a sparkling tiara and sheer veil that dropped to the floor. 'You look incredible. Pete's going to pass out when he sees you.'

Ebony rolled her eyes. 'Let's hope not. It's taken too much effort to get him this far and I'll be damned if he backs out now.'

'Hey, there's no chance of that. My dorky brother's head-over-heels. Are you sure you want to become part of our crazy family?'

To her amazement, a sheen of tears glistened in Ebony's eyes. Her friend rarely cried; in fact, she could probably count the number of times that Ebony had let her emotions get the better of her. 'We're already family, Sis, and don't you forget it.'

Sam hugged her best friend and blinked back

her own tears, knowing that if she let them fall now, she'd never stop. Since her return from Melbourne and in the privacy of her room each night, she'd cried enough tears to fill the Pacific twice over and she'd be damned if she let her own heartbreak spoil Ebony and Pete's wedding day.

Ebony pulled away and bustled into her room. 'OK, time to get this show on the road. There's a chapel not far from here where Prince Charming is waiting.'

Sam chuckled, unable to associate the brother who had put frogs in her bed with Ebony's version of Prince Charming. 'If you say so. Though personally, I think that guy's a fable, ranking alongside Hansel and Gretel and that damned gingerbread house that I spent years searching our local rainforest for as a kid.'

'They're not all like Dylan, you know,' Ebony said, fixing her with a pointed stare.

Sam shrugged, wishing her friend hadn't brought up the subject of the man she'd been trying so desperately to forget. 'It's not his fault. I lied to him. It's natural he'd jump to conclusions about the rest of it.'

'If the man had half a brain in his head he would've followed you up here and given you a chance to explain. Don't you dare defend him!'

Sam squeezed Ebony's arm and led her to the door. 'Calm down. It isn't good for the bride to get this riled before the ceremony. Besides, Dylan Harmon is history. Let's focus on more important matters, like getting you married off.'

Thankfully, Ebony dropped the subject, leaving Sam to wonder how long it would take before she believed her own propaganda and relegated the memory of the one man she loved to past history.

After a week of endless business problems Dylan had finally managed to arrange a flight to Brisbane. He'd had to cancel the trip several times, leading him to believe that perhaps he wasn't destined to sort out the mess with Sam. However, he couldn't get her out of his mind and he knew he owed it to himself to find closure, one way or the other. He wanted answers to several unanswered questions and Sam was the only woman who could provide them.

Striding to the front door of the Popov mansion, he took in the sweeping river views, the manicured lawns and the impressive façade of the entrance, wondering for the hundredth time why a woman with this much wealth would want to marry him just for his money. There had to be more behind her scheme and he wouldn't leave Brisbane till he had all the answers.

He squared his shoulders and thumped on the door, slightly out of his depth for the first time in years and not relishing the feeling one bit.

As the door opened he fixed a smile on his face. However, the response he got wasn't quite what he'd expected.

'What the hell are you doing here?'

CHAPTER TWELVE

DYLAN held out his hand, hoping the other man wouldn't punch him on the nose, which was exactly what he looked as if he would do.

'Hi, Peter. I'm Dylan Harmon. We met at the airport in Sydney, when your sister was working for me?'

Peter stared at him as if he was pond scum and ignored his outstretched hand. 'I remember. Now answer my question. What are you doing here?'

He let his hand drop, wondering where the other man's animosity had sprung from. Surely he was the one who'd been wronged in this whole fiasco? Though with Sam's penchant for lying, who knew what story she'd given her family, which would certainly account for her brother's antagonistic behaviour now.

'I've come to see Sam. Is she here?'

To his surprise, Peter laughed. 'No, she isn't. She stayed at a hotel last night before heading to the chapel. Besides, haven't you left all this a bit late?'

Dylan's heart plummeted as the words penetrated his brain and he took in Peter's tuxedo. Surely Sam wasn't getting married?

Suddenly, the image of Sam and that old man they'd bumped into at the hotel in Sydney sprang to mind and it took all his willpower not to shake the truth out of her smug-looking brother. Dammit, she'd told him her parents had been trying to marry her off to that old fool. What if he'd been stupid enough to push her right into another man's arms?

'Where's the chapel?' He fixed Peter with a stony stare, hoping he'd get the message.

Peter shook his head. 'Oh no, you don't. There's no way you're going to disrupt this day. Just go away and leave my sister alone. She doesn't want to see you.'

Fury surged through Dylan's body, rooting him to the spot. He had to see Sam one last time, even if it was to tell her that she was making the biggest mistake of her life. Hell, she should be marrying him, not some sleazy old man and he'd be damned if he let this wedding go ahead.

He clenched and unclenched his fists, trying to calm down and knowing that what he said in the next few minutes could very well decide his fate. 'I love her,' he finally blurted out, the words scaring him more than he cared to admit.

To his amazement, Peter's expression changed

in an instant and he slapped him on the back. 'Why didn't you say so? Come on, you can ride to the chapel with me. Let's go.'

The limousine ride to the chapel was the longest in Dylan's entire life. He barely listened to Peter's small talk, his mind fixed on the image of Sam in a bridal dress being joined to old Max, whose name he'd finally remembered, in holy matrimony. The thought made him physically ill and he'd downed the several drinks Peter had handed him before he realised that he'd need a completely sober head if he was to convince Sam that she would be making the biggest mistake of her life if she married Max.

The car had barely pulled up when Dylan threw open the door and sprinted for the chapel.

'Hey, what's the hurry? There's plenty of time for you two to talk after the ceremony,' Peter yelled out, only serving to fuel Dylan's urgency.

Had the man lost his mind? After the ceremony would be too late and he'd be damned if he let the best thing that had happened to him slip through his fingers.

Guests stared at him as he ran through the grounds and burst into the chapel. Thankfully, Sam wasn't standing at the altar as he'd envisaged, though his relief was short-lived as a minister strolled down the aisle towards him.

'You're looking for the bride?'

Dylan nodded, swallowing the bitterness that arose at the thought of Sam shortly taking her place in front of that altar without him. 'Is she here?'

The minister pointed to a small room near the entrance. 'She's in there, looking absolutely radiant. I've seen a few brides in my time, but this one—'

'Thanks.' Dylan left the minister gaping as he ran towards the heavy mahogany door and pushed it open without knocking. His heart clenched at the sight of the woman in a beautiful wedding dress standing by the window, though the sunlight streaming through the stained glass window blinded him for a moment.

'Sam, we need to talk.' He strode into the room, determined to talk sense into her and stop this farcical wedding.

'Well, you won't find her here. She's taking a walk by the river.'

Dylan's jaw dropped as the woman by the window turned and walked towards him. 'Ebony? What the hell are you doing, all dressed up like that?'

Ebony rolled her eyes. 'I'm getting married, stupid. And this is what brides wear.'

'*You're* getting married?' Dylan stared at her as if she'd lost her mind. 'But what about Sam? And Max?'

'What about them?' The corners of Ebony's mouth twitched, leaving Dylan with the distinct urge to wipe the smirk off her face.

'Peter led me to believe that Sam was getting married today…' He trailed off, wondering if he'd jumped to conclusions yet again.

Ebony's smirk softened to a smile as she led him to the door and gave him a none-too-gentle shove. 'Why don't you go and find Sam? I think you two need to talk.'

He nodded, suddenly filled with a wild, unrestrained hope that maybe all wasn't lost. Following a winding path to the river, he spotted Sam sitting on a bench. His eyes drank in the sight of her like a thirst-starved man; she looked incredible, wearing a soft-flowing pink halter gown that accentuated her delicate blonde colouring, her curls loose around her shoulders and blowing gently in the breeze.

His reaction was instantaneous and purely visceral. He wanted this woman—no, he *needed* this woman—more than he'd ever needed anyone before. And he wouldn't leave here without her.

Sam glanced at her watch, knowing it was time to head back to the chapel yet reluctant to leave the tranquillity of the river. She took a deep breath, filled with a sense of calm that she rarely found anywhere else. The outback had a similar effect on her, though she quickly pushed that thought from her mind. It reminded her of Budgeree and dredged up a whole host of memories she could do without.

As she stood and brushed down her skirt a shadow fell across her.

'Hello, Sam.'

Her head snapped up at the sound of Dylan's voice and she resisted the urge to collapse back on to the bench. 'What are you doing here?'

'I came to see you.'

She stared at him in disbelief, hardly recognising the dishevelled man before her. What had happened to the suave, sophisticated Dylan Harmon she'd been stupid enough to fall in love with? This man bore little resemblance to him, with dark circles under his eyes indicating that sleep was a distant memory, his suit crumpled and the top button of his shirt undone with the tie awry. She'd never seen him like this and, for a brief moment, hoped he'd had as rough a time as she had over the last week.

She shook her head. 'You've wasted your time.'

'I don't think so. There's too much that needs to be said.'

She squinted up at him, suddenly wishing she hadn't left her sunglasses in the car. The last thing she needed was for him to read the hope, the yearning, in her eyes. 'I thought you'd said it all in Melbourne.' She folded her arms, remembering his accusations and the way he'd crushed her heart. 'Besides, aren't you nervous that I might be out to steal your precious fortune?'

He sat down and patted the seat next to him. 'Why didn't you tell me you were a princess?'

Her eyebrows shot up. 'Who told you that?' She perched on the edge of the bench, as far away from Dylan as possible. She could already smell his familiar cologne and her traitorous body had responded in ways it shouldn't have.

'Mum.' He paused for a moment, as if gathering his thoughts, and she resisted the urge to reach over and smooth away the frown that seemed permanently etched in his brow. 'Why didn't you tell me? And why the name change? Why work for me?' He shook his head. 'It just doesn't make any sense.'

Guilt filled her. She should never have involved him in her scheme to make her parents see sense. 'If I'd told you my history, I wouldn't have been hired. And I needed the job, desperately.'

'But why? You have all the money in the world.' He stared at her as if she'd lost her mind.

'It wasn't about the money.' She took a steadying breath, hoping he would understand. 'I've told you about my parents' expectations?' His slight nod encouraged her to continue. 'Well, it went deeper than that. They were so caught up in the traditions of their heritage that they made my life hell when I was growing up. I just had to buck the system and the only way I could think of was to prove to them that I could make it on my own in the world, without their influence or money.'

Despite her explanation, she caught the puzzled gleam in his eyes. 'Then why mention marriage to me?'

Sam swallowed, realising she'd have to be extremely careful in answering his question if she didn't want to reveal too much about her true feelings. 'What you overheard that day was a joke. Ebony is my best friend, she was in on the plan from the start, which is why she gave your mother a false reference. She also knew that I'd lied to my parents and told them that the reason I was going to Melbourne was to further a relationship with you. I was merely discussing that with her.'

An uncomfortable silence ensued and she wished he would say something, anything, to break the growing tension.

'What about the rest?'

'The rest?' She pretended not to understand the question, when in fact she knew exactly what Dylan referred to and the mere thought of it set her heart pounding.

'What happened at Budgeree. Was that just part of an act too?'

He'd given her the perfect opportunity to end it all, right here, right now. All she had to do was answer in the affirmative and she knew he'd walk out of her life for good. Sure, he'd accepted her explanation for lying to him about her work, but which man would tolerate a woman faking affection when it came to the bedroom?

She opened her mouth to say yes but couldn't do it. Despite everything that had happened and her week of self-indoctrination that she didn't love him, she couldn't lie to him about this.

'Sam?'

She heard the uncertainty in his voice and it undid the last of her fleeting resistance. Looking up, she stared him straight in the eye. 'No, that wasn't an act.'

His eyes burned with some indefinable emotion and darkened to almost black. 'Then what was it?'

No matter how much she loved him, she couldn't admit it. So what if he'd come up here? He still hadn't told her why and she'd be damned if she made a complete fool of herself by admitting her feelings.

Crossing her fingers in her lap and hoping she wouldn't get struck down for such a monstrous lie, she answered, 'I was attracted to you and assumed the feeling was mutual. We'd been flirting for a while, so it seemed natural to take it to the next level.'

'That's it?'

She schooled her features into a mask of indifference and shrugged. 'What else could it be?'

He paled slightly beneath his tan and she almost felt sorry for him. 'Uh…I thought you might have feelings for me.'

'Feelings?' She laughed, a bitter sound that did little to soothe the pain in her heart. Seeing Dylan again had resurrected her barely suppressed love for him, hearing him talk about feelings was proving to be too much. 'Come on, Dylan, we both know that would be disastrous.'

'Why?' He pinned her with a probing stare and she tried not to squirm.

'We're too different. I'm trying to escape the shackles of my family, you're so wound up in family responsibilities you can't see straight.'

His eyes widened a fraction, drawing her into their seductive depths. 'What's that supposed to mean?'

And suddenly she knew how to put an end to all this pain, all the heartache. 'From what I've heard, it doesn't take a genius to figure out you're carrying some huge chip on your shoulder because of your dad. Is that why you're so protective of the Harmon fortune?' There, she'd done it, hit him where he was most vulnerable. Surely he'd leave her alone now?

He stood up and thrust his hands in his pockets, anger radiating off him in waves, unable to meet her gaze. 'Sorry to have bothered you.'

'No bother. See you round.'

He didn't respond and she watched him walk away, her heart breaking all over again.

CHAPTER THIRTEEN

'YOU'RE crazy, no doubt about it.'

Sam stared at Ebony, surprised at her friend's vehement reaction. 'Thanks for the vote of confidence. You sure know how to kick a woman when she's down.'

The wedding and reception had gone off without a hitch, despite Sam's constant battle to hold back the waterworks. Now, as she helped her friend change into her 'going away' outfit, she'd finally told her what had happened with Dylan earlier. What she hadn't counted on was Ebony's reaction.

'Are you that thick? Can't you see the man's in love with you?'

Sam snorted. 'Yeah, right. That's why he went down on bended knee and professed his undying passion.' She turned away and busied herself with hanging Ebony's beautiful dress, wishing she could erase the dream of Dylan doing exactly that from her mind.

Ebony grabbed her arm. 'Did you give him a chance?'

Sam looked away, unable to meet her friend's

probing stare. 'What for? It's hopeless. We're too different.'

'See? What did I tell you? Crazy, with a capital C!'

Sam shook free of her grasp, blinking back tears for the hundredth time that day. 'Take it easy, Eb. I don't need this right now.'

Ebony shimmied into her skirt and zipped up, giving Sam time to compose herself. At least her friend hadn't turned into a heartless monster completely. However, her relief was short-lived.

'Look, I shouldn't be telling you this but you need to know. The worst thing you could've said to Dylan was accusing him of carrying around some baggage about his father.'

'Why?' By the sombre expression on her friend's face, Sam didn't want to know the answer.

'Because he *is* caught up on some weird guilt trip where his dad is concerned. His dad died while Dylan was overseas, kicking up his heels and shunning his family responsibilities.'

Just like her. The thought sprang to Sam's mind and she couldn't shake it. What if one of her parents had died while she'd been hiding in Melbourne? She would probably feel the same guilt Dylan did and would try to make up for it the best way she knew how. Was that what drove the man? It more than explained his ties to Budgeree and his distaste for her views on family that she'd expressed there.

Sam shook her head from side to side. 'I've made a huge mistake, haven't I?'

'Colossal!' Ebony guided her towards the door. 'Now, go after him.'

'To Melbourne?' Sam doubted she had the courage to fly down there and confront the man she'd hurt so much. Besides, what if her friend's assumptions were right and he did love her? Could that be possible? And, if so, what could she do about it to win him back?

Ebony grinned, the same cheeky smile Sam had grown to recognise meant 'trouble' over the years. 'No, silly. The man had enough class to come back to the chapel and wish me good luck after you'd broken his heart down by the river. And I managed to find out where he was staying tonight, just in case you'd botched things up, which his hangdog expression told me you had. So, go to the Marriott and start grovelling!'

Sam hugged her friend. 'What would I do without you?'

'Probably make a total hotchpotch of your life. Now go!' Ebony squeezed her back, before practically shoving her out the door.

* * *

Dylan turned off the taps and stepped from the shower, wishing the steamy blast of hot water had done more to soothe his aching body. He'd had a week of sleepless nights thanks to his obsession with Sam, tossing and turning till the wee hours. The flight to Brisbane hadn't helped. The only seat available had been economy and he wasn't used to folding his long legs into such cramped quarters.

To make matters worse, the entire trip had been a waste of time and he couldn't wait to return to Melbourne and put the whole sordid business behind him.

A tentative knock sounded at the door and he cursed whoever had the audacity to disrupt him tonight of all nights. He needed sleep, sleep and more sleep, which only the anonymity of a hotel room could provide.

Wrapping a towel around his waist, he padded across the plush carpet and wrenched open the door. 'Yes?'

Sam stood there, doing her utmost not to stare at his chest and failing miserably. It reminded him of the day they'd first met in his bedroom, when he'd seen the flicker of interest in her eyes despite her attempts to hide it. However, he wouldn't be so foolish this time—and he just had to hope that his body would respond accordingly.

'Can I come in?' Her voice came out in a whisper and for one insane moment, despite all that had happened and all that she'd said, he wanted to reach out and envelop her in his arms.

'I'm going to bed.' Unfortunately, his words conjured up visions of taking her with him and a certain part of his anatomy responded in predictable fashion.

'This won't take long.' She stared at him, her green eyes pleading. He'd never seen her like this and, despite his intentions to push her away, it shook him.

'Fine. But make it snappy.' He opened the door wider and gestured her in, trying to ignore the waft of floral perfume that enveloped him in a sensuous cloud as she came in. Rather than gaining control of his libido, his body flared with desire at the familiar scent and he mentally chastised himself for still wanting her.

She strolled to the window and looked at the view before squaring her shoulders and turning to face him. 'I came here to apologise.'

'Too late for that, isn't it?' No matter what she said now, it wouldn't make one iota of difference. He'd resolved to forget this woman and throw himself into what he knew best—making his family business flourish.

'I hope not.' She stood there, staring at him with those sad eyes, beseeching him to listen. 'I shouldn't have said those things about your father. I was way out of line and hope you'll forgive me.'

'Just forget it.' He waved away her apology as if it meant nothing. Words were useless at a time like this. Too much had happened for them to mean much.

'Please, let me finish.' She plucked at a loose thread on her gown and he suddenly wished the whole gossamer-thin thing would unravel before his eyes. Just another indication of how sleep-deprived he actually was. 'I know how you feel—'

'Give me a break!' His patience finally snapped. 'You have no idea how I feel. I was like you once, trying to shirk family responsibilities with every fibre of my being. And you know what happened? It killed my dad.' He stalked towards her, wishing she'd stop staring at him with pity in her eyes. 'I couldn't wait to escape, especially Budgeree. My dad would rave on for hours about how that piece of land would be the crowning jewel in the Harmon fortune and, all that time, I would listen and nod and plan my life away from it. So I did it. I left Dad, his pipe dreams and the whole damn lot behind me and didn't look back. And what happened? The pressure of running the business alone killed him. *I* killed him,' he shouted, willing her to listen. The sight of tears welling in her eyes did little to calm him.

He turned away from her, wishing she'd get the hell out of his life. He hadn't meant to tell her all that; it'd spilled out, leaving him strangely relieved. She'd been the first person he'd ever voiced those feelings to, though he knew his mum suspected how he felt.

'Don't you think he would've wanted you to live a little before taking on such a huge responsibility?'

'How would you know what he wanted? You weren't there. You didn't see the disappointment in his eyes the day I told him I was going away, with no idea of when I'd be back.' The pain of that memory had eaten away at Dylan for more years than he cared to remember, though he'd done his best to make up for it by shouldering the family responsibilities on his return.

'Your mum told me.'

'Told you what?'

'How your dad felt when you went away. We discussed it that first day when I told her my family secrets.'

Dylan turned around and stared at her, wanting to hear the truth yet wishing they'd never started this conversation. 'Tell me. Though why Mum would confide in you, the queen of deception, is beyond me.'

She ignored his barb, though he noted a downward turn of her lips. 'He loved you, more than you ever knew. He was so proud that you'd stayed around so long to learn the ropes from him and he hoped that you'd return one day to continue his dream. He never begrudged you that time away, nor did he kill himself trying to make up for your absence. Heart attacks happen for a lot of reasons and he died doing what he loved best, running the family business.' She paused to wipe away a lone tear that trickled down her cheek. 'Your mum said she's tried to tell you this several times but you always change the subject, so she decided to leave well enough alone. Though I think it's time you sat down with her and had a long chat about your dad, don't you?'

Rather than Sam's tears abating, as he'd expected once she'd finished her spiel, they now flowed unchecked, leaving him at a loss.

'Save the tears, Sam. I don't need your sympathy.' He turned his back on her and strolled towards the window, wishing she would leave him the hell alone. He needed to assimilate what she'd just told him, to sort out his feelings where his family was concerned.

'If you don't want my sympathy, what about my love?'

The whispered words slammed home, though it took him a good ten seconds to register their meaning.

'What did you say?' He jumped as she slid her arms around his waist and pressed her face against his back.

'I love you,' she said, squeezing him so tightly he could hardly breathe. Or was that the overwhelming sensation of disbelief that had him struggling for air?

He loosened her grip and turned to face her, searching for the right words and failing miserably.

Sam took a steadying breath and continued before she lost the last of her courage. 'I know you probably don't want to hear this, but I lied to you earlier. Again. What happened at Budgeree between us was proof of how I feel about you. I fell in love with you almost from the beginning but didn't want to admit it and when I thought our time together was drawing to a close, I wanted to take away some lasting memory of our time together.'

'So, you used me for sex?' To her delight, a

slow smile crept across his face, the same killer smile she'd grown to love and she knew in that moment that she had a chance to win him back.

'I wouldn't call it using.' She allowed her hands to play over his back, raking the bare skin lightly with her nails. 'Call it a mutually satisfying arrangement.'

He growled in response and pulled her close, his lips crushing hers in a scorching kiss. Her tongue snaked out to meet his, teasing, tasting, and she wanted him with a ferocity that was staggering. She'd thought that she would never have this chance again, so she'd thrown caution to the wind and admitted her true feelings. She loved Dylan Harmon and wanted to shout it to the world.

He leaned into her, the evidence of his arousal sending a sudden flood of pleasure rushing through her and with a slow, deliberate movement she ground her hips against his. He broke the kiss, staring at her with undisguised lust and more than a hint of confusion. 'You do know I love you too?'

As her body throbbed with powerful, soul-wrenching need, her mind managed to assimilate what he'd just said and she smiled, a seductive upturning of her lips designed to entice. 'Show me.'

EPILOGUE

SAM stared into the growing darkness and tried to ignore the faint niggle of apprehension in her gut. Dylan should have returned an hour ago and, despite his extensive knowledge of Budgeree and its surrounding lands, she couldn't help but worry. Even though they spent most of their time here, she knew the outback held a multitude of hidden dangers cleverly disguised by its raw, unadulterated beauty.

Turning away from the window, she busied herself with making a cup of tea, anything to take her mind off the absence of her husband.

Her husband.

Even after a year, the thought of Dylan Harmon being entirely hers still brought a smile to her face and a heated flush to her cheeks. They'd been married here at Budgeree, surrounded by family, in a quiet affair as they both had wanted. She still worked as his personal assistant, though some of the tasks in her job description seemed more *personal* than others—and she loved every minute of it.

She wandered out to the veranda and sat in her favourite rocking chair, cradling the mug of tea in her hands. Outback nights could plunge to subzero temperatures and tonight would prove to be no exception.

All the better to cuddle up with someone warm… Dylan's words popped into her mind and she took a sip of tea, wishing he'd appear.

She finished her tea and started rocking, the gentle motion soothing her.

'Wake up, Sleeping Beauty. Time to give your husband the welcome home he deserves.'

Sam jumped as Dylan brushed her lips with a feather-light kiss, not realising she'd managed to doze. She leaped from the chair and wrapped her arms around him, snuggling into the warmth of his body, breathing in the intoxicating mix of male sweat, horse and pure Dylan. 'Where have you been?'

He hugged her tight, stroking her hair away from her face. 'Working. You know, that thing I do for a living. Missed me, huh?'

'Come here, Wiseguy.' She pulled his head down and kissed him, her throat growing thick with the emotion she now recognised as true love.

'Now *that's* what I call a homecoming,' he murmured against the side of her mouth, his hands pulling her flush against him.

She pulled away slightly and quirked an eyebrow. 'Stick with me, honey, and you'll go places.'

'Is that so?' He twisted a curl around his finger and gently tugged on it, drawing her towards him again, his gaze firmly fixed on her lips.

She nodded, basking in the love they shared. 'So, think you can handle being married to royalty?' It was a question she often teased him with, knowing the answer before he opened his mouth to respond.

'With you by my side, Princess, I can handle anything.'

And he swept her into his arms and strode into the homestead to prove it.

MILLS & BOON®

Live the emotion

Tender romance™

THE AUSTRALIAN TYCOON'S PROPOSAL
by Margaret Way *(The Australians)*

Bronte's had enough of rich, ruthless men – she's just escaped marrying one! So she's wary when tycoon Steven Randolph arrives on her doorstep with a business proposal, especially as she finds him impossible to resist. Only then she discovers that Steven is not all he seems…

CHRISTMAS EVE MARRIAGE by Jessica Hart

The only thing Thea was looking for on holiday was a little R & R – she didn't expect to find herself roped into being Rhys Kingsford's pretend fiancée! Being around Rhys was exciting, exhilarating…in fact he was everything Thea ever wanted. But back home reality sank in. Perhaps it was just a holiday fling…?

THE DATING RESOLUTION by Hannah Bernard

After a series of failed relationships, Hailey's made a resolution: no dating, no flirting, no men for an entire year! But what happens when you're six months in to your no dating year and you meet temptation himself? Jason Halifax is sinfully sexy and lives right next door. What's a girl to do?

THE GAME SHOW BRIDE by Jackie Braun *(9 to 5)*

Kelli Walters wants a better life – even if that means participating in a reality TV game show. She has to swap lives and jobs with vice president Sam Maxwell – telling people what to do while he has to scrape by as a single mum! But Sam soon ups the stakes with his heart-stopping smiles and smouldering glances!

On sale 5th November 2004

Available at most branches of WHSmith, Tesco, ASDA, Martins, Borders, Eason, Sainsbury's and all good paperback bookshops.

A story of passions and betrayals...
and the dangerous obsessions they spawn

PENNY
JORDAN
SILVER

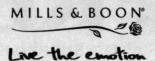

MILLS & BOON®

Live the emotion

Next month don't miss –

PREGNANT BRIDES

The Fatherhood Affair *by Emma Darcy*
Expecting His Baby *by Sandra Field*
Dr Carlisle's Child *by Carol Marinelli*

*Take one gorgeous hero, add one
beautiful heroine, throw in some
passion…emotion…a pregnancy…
a wedding…a lot of love…
The result? PARENTHOOD!*

On sale 5th November 2004

*Available at most branches of WHSmith, Tesco, ASDA, Martins,
Borders, Eason, Sainsbury's and all good paperback bookshops.*

1004/05

4 FREE

BOOKS AND A SURPRISE GIFT!

We would like to take this opportunity to thank you for reading this Mills & Boon® book by offering you the chance to take FOUR more specially selected titles from the Tender Romance™ series absolutely FREE! We're also making this offer to introduce you to the benefits of the Reader Service™—

- ★ **FREE home delivery**
- ★ **FREE gifts and competitions**
- ★ **FREE monthly Newsletter**
- ★ **Exclusive Reader Service offers**
- ★ **Books available before they're in the shops**

Accepting these FREE books and gift places you under no obligation to buy, you may cancel at any time, even after receiving your free shipment. Simply complete your details below and return the entire page to the address below. You don't even need a stamp!

YES! Please send me 4 free Tender Romance books and a surprise gift. I understand that unless you hear from me, I will receive 6 superb new titles every month for just £2.69 each, postage and packing free. I am under no obligation to purchase any books and may cancel my subscription at any time. The free books and gift will be mine to keep in any case.

N4ZED

Ms/Mrs/Miss/Mr ....Initials ....

BLOCK CAPITALS PLEASE

Surname ....

Address ....

....

....Postcode.............................

Send this whole page to:
UK: FREEPOST CN81, Croydon, CR9 3WZ